TOO MANY DOCTORS

TOO MANY DOCTORS

HOLLY ROTH

WILDSIDE PRESS

For Jo

With my love

TOO MANY DOCTORS

MONDAY

The M. S. *Tilburg* had anchored off Cowes to pick up its Southampton cargo and passengers, in that order.

The passengers—ten of them, which would make a round total of fifty when they were stowed away with those who had already boarded at Hamburg, Bremen, and Rotterdam—were finally permitted to slog their way off the wet dock and up the slippery gangplank to the tender. That was at 11:05 A.M.

The tender chugged through Southampton Water past the Isle of Wight, and, at 11:55 A.M. rounded the port side of the *Tilburg* where it lay patiently at anchor. The passengers, defending themselves against the wet wind with scarves and yanked-down hats, crawled to the tender's top deck and up the gangplank of the *Tilburg* itself. Then they were herded still farther upward to the Promenade Deck and into the lounge, where the green and gold furnishings looked elegant and the oriental fernery ridiculously exotic against the newcomers' drab wetness and the lowering grayness of the sea- and landscape that formed the lounge's fore window wall. The formalities of relinquishing passports and boarding cards and answering the few questions put by the purser took fifteen minutes, and that was all the third officer, working his men furiously under the frenzied eye of the chief officer, needed to get the crated baggage hoisted aboard. Both the chief and the third mate happened to be unusually sweet-tempered men, but by law, custom, and immediate circumstance they were under the influence of the captain, and the captain was of a different temperament. The captain's normally uneven disposition was constantly tilted to wild slants by the impossibility of handling gently both passengers and cargo, and of maneuvering "eleven seas, three oceans, eight straits, nine bays, four gulfs, and one canal" (thus ran his bitter litany whenever he was in his cups, which he entered regularly each morning at breakfast) "—*and back again*—all in a period of four months, and keeping to a schedule." The *Tilburg* was already a day behind that schedule at Southampton and not one-eighth of the total period had elapsed.

The indirect result of the captain's disposition was that, by the time the new passengers had progressed to the point of going below and sorting out their cabin luggage and staterooms, the *Tilburg* was revving up its motors and winching up its anchor. But she had not yet moved, was sitting steady as a rock in the sullen, rain-chastened waters, when the woman fell down the stairs.

From the Promenade Deck down to A Deck there wound a wide, curving flight of stairs, fifteen in all. On the wall side a handrail followed the wall's concavity; the outer railing was formed of a low Plexiglass sweep, an open parabola that permitted one to see from one deck to another. The staircase, in its modernity and with its swooping sides, was graceful, happily designed; it was also as safe as a staircase can be. Nevertheless the woman fell, and she fell with force, as if she had hurled herself down the fifteen steps. That was about a quarter of an hour after noon on Monday, January 14th.

4

TUESDAY

SCHIFF *Tilburg*
SHIP

Dienstag den *15* ten *Januar*
Tuesday the of *January*
46° 58'N Breite und *06° 21'W* Länge
Latitude and Longitude

Tages-Distanz: *290* Seemeilen
Day's run: Nautical miles

Zurückgelegte Gesamtdistanz bis heute: *290*
Total distance covered up to today:

Restdistanz bis: *Genua*
Distance still to be covered to: *1680 mi*

By two-thirty on Tuesday afternoon, when he stood rolling and pitching on the Promenade Deck, clutching at a doorframe and trying to synchronize his vision with the report of the ship's run toward its next port of call, Max Owings had got a fair idea of the *Tilburg*'s physical layout and statistics. She was motor-driven ("M. S." stood for "Motor Schiff") as opposed to steam-driven—a fact that was incessantly noticeable. Her two Diesels were not synchronized, and their alternate thuddings were drumlike to the tympanum of the ear and a punishment to the flesh. The fact that she was rolling like an advanced drunk and pitching like a hobbyhorse might have been put down to the vagaries of the infamous Bay of Biscay, but Max felt certain that the thump-thump of those unharnessed engines was likely to be with them for weeks to come.

The *Tilburg* was a German ship, her home port being Hamburg. She was 518½ feet long overall, 61 feet across the beam, and had a draft of 25½. Her speed was reported to be 17 knots, but from the feel of the engines Max regarded that figure with a skepticism unsupported by either engineering or nautical knowledge. She carried a crew of eighty-eight, and boasted eighty-seven passenger beds, and on the two other trips she made each year—the purser had so advised Max at the luncheon table half an hour before—every bed was usually booked. But this was the winter trip, and the purser admitted that not only were there a mere fifty aboard, fifteen of them children, but that the number would diminish before they reached Japan since people would disembark along the way. He added sadly that during the other eight months they picked up rather than lost people in Hong Kong and Singapore and Sarawak and Manila. He had a face like a thin old horse, and Max wondered if the sadness was merely hide deep, an expression rather than a sentiment. Max had a sudden notion that the purser's prevailing emotion was something quite different, something more like fear.

"And the engines?" Max asked him. "Are they always out of synch like this?"

The purser's long bony face looked cautious. "Perhaps. Just a little."

"A little?" Max's smile was, as usual, gentle and sardonic at the same time. "Like a little garlic, a little pregnant, a little war?"

"*Ach, so?*" said the purser, and galloped off, leaving his coffee untouched.

Well, Max thought, as he wandered through the seemingly empty ship a couple of hours later, the humor had been pretty tired, God knows, but a "little" out of synchronization had torn the clichés from him. Was it simply Germanic stodginess that had sent the purser stampeding away? Or fear of the word "war"? Max wondered if the tall sad purser had a small mad wife, or if it was the icily handsome captain he was afraid of, and then he thought of the thousand and one other sources of men's fears. And frowned. The habit of amateurish psychoanalyzing—sheer unsupported guesswork reminiscent of witch-doctoring—was a bad one. He must stop it.

But he didn't.

He had had four meals on the *Tilburg* so far: lunch and dinner the day before, breakfast and lunch on this, the second day out of Southampton. And at all the meals the atmosphere had been—peculiar. Max examined the word, and found it unsupportable. The lunch he had just been offered, for instance, had been enormous and, for the first time, well attended. Now it seemed that everyone except himself was either sleeping off the weight of it, or struggling with the fairly predictable seasickness brought on by it. (Max, armed with the knowledge that man cannot know himself, not even physically, had drunk clear broth and eaten a medium-sized, medium-cooked steak.)

. . . But something peculiar was going on. Could it be himself? Or rather, the passengers' reaction to Max Owings? He shook his head slightly, examined the cold-looking sea through the windows of the deserted lounge, felt as desolate as it looked, and told himself not to be a self-conscious fool. Most of these people had probably never heard of him. And at any rate, the reaction to him, so far as he had experienced it before he boarded, was not fear but contempt and disgust. The fear was more likely in himself. Well, no sense in dwelling . . .

Forgetting that there could be no reason for mass fright (unless the woman's fall the day before had unnerved them?), they were as diverse a group of people as one could assemble. Take, for instance, his table companions . . .

Huddling his thin frame into his suede jacket, Max strolled out onto the aft deck and nodded at the first person he had seen in a quarter-hour, a tall healthy young deckhand who was swabbing the deck. Then Max sat down beside the shining dry swimming pool and took his table companions, one by one.

They were five at table. There was the sad, bony purser, a Mr. and Mrs. Pitkethly, a Mr. Clarkson, and Max himself. They had all boarded at Southampton with the exception, of course, of the purser. The purser was German, as probably were all of the officers and crew. Mr. Pitkethly turned out to be a Scot. He was a short, middle-aged man, physically powerful, vaguely ape-ish. Under his too tight suit jacket muscles strained and bunched as if bidding for freedom. Despite the width of his shoulders and the roundhouse proportions of his chest, his head was big by comparison. All of that massive head—hair, large mustache, eyebrows, mouth, and skin—was a dark, turbulent red. Max diagnosed high blood pressure.

Mr. Pitkethly's nationality had not been immediately clear. In the beginning Max caught nothing the man said the first time, and sometimes not the second. Pitkethly finally took pity on him. "Don't worrry about not underrstandin'. Ye'll ketch it in time. I'm a Glaswegian."

A glass-what? Max thought, stifling a desire to laugh. He thought wildly of ouija boards.

"From Glasgow," Pitkethly added helpfully, "and the Glaswegian accent is a bit thick, or so I'm told by the English." So the Greek-to-Max speech was Scottish.

Mrs. Pitkethly, a tiny Japanese, spoke little. When she did, however, she too caused some strain because she exhibited her countrymen's frequent confusion of l's and r's. Also, she whispered sibilantly. Mrs. Pitkethly had none of the advertised mysteriousness of the East; she was scared to death and she showed it. Her husband went out of his way to soothe her. (Max frowned; it should have been touching. Why did he find it not at all so? Was he as callous as the world thought him?) Mr. Pitkethly's huge red face—wrinkled, full of up lines—should have radiated good nature but it didn't even achieve warmth. He kept it bent steadily over the minute head of his wife, a homely little woman with small darting eyes who bore one family resemblance to her husband: she looked like a rhesus monkey.

Mr. Clarkson, the fifth member, was a tall, stocky Englishman with a softer accent than most. He was probably sixty, making a still-handsome entry into old age. His face, too, was red, but unlike Mr. Pitkethly's it was a clear pink-red, glowingly healthy and hearty. Until the purser had fled, followed shortly thereafter by a scurrying Mrs. Pitkethly, Max had thought him rather a benevolent type. But, once alone with Pitkethly and Max, it developed that Clarkson had swallowed a sewer immediately before lunch, and was determined to vomit it back at them.

"You're American, eh?" he said to Max.

Max admitted it.

"Only one aboard, so far's I know. One of the very few I've ever met. Although since I've been traveling on these ships for the better part of twenty years, and lived in the East all that time, I've known a pretty diverse group. Well, what are they like in America?"

Max examined that and found it too big for him. "Like?" he said. "People?"

"Babes." Coming out of the bland pink face, the word was madly inappropriate. Max choked.

Pitkethly helped him out. "Like babes everywhere, I suppose. Except, of course, my wife."

Max's head swiveled. That was the damndest sentence he'd heard in a long time. Gentlemen, the babe whom I have the honor to call my wife is not a babe. All other babes—

Clarkson said, "You're probably right. Bunch of tramps. Take the gal on the captain's right, which I wouldn't mind doing." He leered benevolently at the captain's table. The woman on the captain's right was an extremely handsome Chinese, smartly dressed in Western clothes. From the rear Max had thought for a moment that she was a fellow-American, but the masses of blue-black, high-coiffed hair had killed the illusion even before he saw the charming long-eyed mask that was her face. "The captain's babe," Clarkson confided. "Rides the ship twice a year. But he takes his leaves in Hamburg. Got a wife there."

"A very pretty woman," Max said. She looked about thirty.

Clarkson plucked his thought and corrected it: "Fifty-two or -three. Name's Hausman. Kam-Ping Hausman."

"Camping?" Max began to feel as if he were never going to touch bottom.

"No, no. Kam-Ping," Clarkson enunciated. "These funny Chinese names are not a Western joke, you know. They really exist. F'rinstance, the chap who does our cargo at Singapore, has the dock contract, y'know, is named Fat Lip. Really. Preposterous name, but a prosperous bloke. Prosperous enough to afford all the four wives and about twelve concubines. He must be good." The leer on Clarkson's bluff face achieved a larger-than-life effect.

Max looked down into his coffee, away from the lascivious grin. He had started off by liking the pink-faced Englishman; now he had come to consider him a dirty-minded gossip. But Max would be on this ship until Hong Kong, almost six weeks hence, and Clarkson might be his table-mate for the whole period. Besides, sometimes things were not as they seemed, as Max damned well knew. And when he looked up at the still-smiling face of Clarkson he realized it was actually possible that Clarkson wasn't a licentious bastard after all. Clarkson had shed the leer and reachieved simple benevolence. He waved his hand at the room in which the two-score people, although mainly British, included Japanese, Chinese, Malayans, an Indian, a Filipino, and a few diverse types that defied immediate definition. "Don't see groups like this in the States, do you?"

Max realized that he had never seen anything quite like such an assortment in one room, certainly not in one room devoted to a social purpose like dining.

Clarkson didn't wait for an answer. He said, "No, I'm sure you don't. You're anti-miscegenation, of course. Like South Africa."

Should he have used the word miscegenation in Pitkethly's presence? Or was it Max who was giving a nasty connotation to a word that was, after all, merely a denotation of a fact? At least the silent Pitkethly looked no redder than usual. "No," Max said. "We're not at all like the South Africans. Only the South is. The Southern part of the United States, that is. And they are not as extreme as the South Africans."

Clarkson looked skeptical and Max, feeling it foolish to be annoyed, was annoyed. Keep it on a level of annoyance, he said to himself, knowing that his spurts of temper were unpredictable and disproportionate to the provocation. He said, keeping his voice dispassionate, "The comparison is often made, of course. Especially by those in authority in South Africa. But it ignores the one great difference. In South Africa, the Government, authority itself, is officially oppressing the vast majority of the population. In the United States the Government is officially attempting to end the oppression of one minority by another minority. Democracy is always inclined to work slowly, but the American Government is succeeding little by little."

"Um. So you're a Northerner?"

"Yes."

"Where in the North?"

Max hesitated, then said reluctantly, "Near Milwaukee." He didn't like to talk about Milwaukee and always hoped he would not meet a Milwaukean.

"And even though America refers to itself, with incomprehensible pride, as a 'melting pot,' you've never seen an assemblage like this?"

Max struggled, not with the answer, which was inescapable, but with the reason for that answer. Then, suddenly, he smiled, and the smile was, as always, unexpectedly warm in his thin, severe face. He said, "Mr. Clarkson, I am a minority on this ship. As you pointed out, I seem to be the only American."

Clarkson smiled too. "Not sporting, huh? I'll give you a tip. Next time an Englishman starts such a baiting, just mention 'the Empire.' Mention of that vanished world leaves him no alternative but to slink off. Another tip. This group of people will eventually seem just like people to you."

"So they do now."

Clarkson shook his head. "Un-uh. Now they seem like a group of mixed races. Eventually they will seem like people, some good, some bad, some bright, some stupid. So forth. That young babe"—he nodded at a far table—"will be simply beautiful."

"And so she is now."

"Ah, but now you think of her as a half-Filipino, half-Malayan beauty. Later, she'll be just a beauty, unless she turns out to be a bitch. Then you'll think of her as a bitch. Not necessarily a mixed-breed bitch. See?"

So, Max thought, that's what the girl is. He caught himself, recognized how right Clarkson had been, and was discomfited to see that Clarkson had followed the thought. Clarkson nodded. He said, "I went through it once."

"You seem to know the route well. You've made it often?"

"The route and even this ship and its officers. Sailed a round trip on her once before, half a dozen years ago. Altogether I've made six round trips. Six and a half when I get there this time. Twenty years now."

"When you get to—?"

"Sarawak." He put the accent on the second syllable and didn't pronounce the "k" at all.

"Oh, then you get off at Miri."

"Not a bit of it. Get off at Singapore."

"Why not Miri? That's in Sarawak, isn't it?"

"Yes, but I'm going to Kuching. Miri is a hellhole, but that's not my reason for avoiding it. Thing is, trip down the coast is impossible by road. *Are* no through roads. Have to take coastal steamers. Hot, hard going. So I disembark Singapore and fly over to Kuching." He turned to Pitkethly. "You, too, I should imagine?"

"We disembark at Miri." Mr. Pitkethly beamed redly.

"But aren't you going to North Borneo?"

"Aye. West of Sandakan. Sago plantation."

"But"—Clarkson looked puzzled—"that's a vicious expedition. Up coast from Miri, along the coast of Brunei, and more than halfway around North Borneo."

"Aye."

"But you could fly from Manila. Or take a steamer from Hong Kong—only a three- or four-day trip."

"Put it doon t' the fact I'm a Scot." The red face wrinkled coldly upward.

"But—your wife is with you."

"Aye."

There was a silence. Max was sitting between the two men, the empty chairs of Mrs. Pitkethly and the purser facing him. During the short silence he became oddly aware that an out-of-place sense of emotion had been generated by the discussion. Was it fear? he thought again, and again decided that the emotion might be purely subjective. But the feeling was strong enough to make him reach for a conversational gambit to break up the moment. He said, "Sago? That's a sort of starch, isn't it?"

"It *is* starch, yes." Pitkethly swung his big head away from Clarkson's steady gaze and peered up at Max.

"There seem to be a lot of plantation people. I've heard rubber mentioned, and tea."

"That's right." Pitkethly nodded. "Rubber people go up north of Kuala Lumpur mostly. Tea people to Ceylon. So forth. There're also pepper, coconut, coffee, and tobacco planters aboard. You're going to Hong Kong, aren't you?"

"Yes."

"Ah, then, you'll come across copra."

"Physically," Clarkson murmured.

Max looked inquiring.

"Come acropper the copra," Clarkson explained. "They usually load the stuff in the Philippine ports."

"We stop only in Manila," Max pointed out.

"According to the schedule," Clarkson agreed. "But these ships invariably stop wherever a copra crop crops up." He laughed and said, "Forgive me; there is nothing funny about copra. Nor about ports like Cebu, for instance."

"Stinks," Mr. Pitkethly said. "The ports and the copra."

"And the copra bug. Sort of a flying beetle. Boat gets thick with them. Very disagreeable."

"Really? But to an American it all seems . . ." Max paused.

Clarkson was smiling. "A bit romantic?"

"Well, Somerset Maugham-ish."

"Logically enough," Clarkson said. "Maugham wrote of the outposts of the Empire. Remnants still exist, and even where they are finished the local inhabitants often discover to their surprise that the British weren't so bad after all, and that their ability—their 'know-how,' as the Americans say—is still valuable. At least until such time as the natives can pick their brains. These people"—he nodded at the emptying room—"still represent outposts. The civilization thereof. They are teachers, civil servants, planters, cable and wireless people, some military. Such like. They've had six-month leaves and now they're returning to outposts where they'll stay for three solid years. That's the most familiar pattern, at any rate."

"I see. And you"—not military, Max thought. Perhaps a civil servant? Most likely a something to do with a plantation. Max could easily picture the pink face, smiling benevolently, looming over a Simon Legree type of whip —"and you, Mr. Clarkson, are you a planter?"

"Me? Oh, no. I divide myself three ways—teach in Kuching mornings, three afternoons a week go down to the Leper Settlement, thirteen miles outside of Kuching, and on week ends tend to the first of my callings—preach. I'm a missionary."

Max looked down at the pool's blue-green tiled bottom, through the heavy net that covered its emptiness in order to protect the unwary. It had had no such net during lunch. He tried mentally to remove the whip from Mr. Clarkson's hand and replace it with a Bible. He found it a difficult feat of evocation. The man was the antithesis of the clerical gentleman to whom Sadie Thompson was Nemesis; the Reverend Mr. Davidson, Maugham had called him. Max wondered idly why Maugham had fallen into the trap of having terminated his two leading characters' names with the same suffix, and realized he was back into Maugham again. The "remnants of the Empire," Clarkson had said. Clark*son*, Max thought, and smiled. So, then, he, Max, had stumbled into the remnants of Maugham. He wondered if Clarkson was called "The Reverend Mr. Clarkson," smiled again, and then, as he thought about names, his smile faded. For no one had asked his name. No one had called him by name or title. No one had asked his profession. Perhaps they knew the answers?

Max Owings heard his name, and brought his gaze up out of the swimming pool.

2

At noon on that Tuesday, the ship's doctor—two wide gold stripes and a caduceus on his sleeve—shut the door of

Cabin 42 behind him and mounted the graceful stairway. He asked directions of a deckhand and then, following instructions, went through a door that wore a sign saying, *Zutritt nicht gestattet. No admittance. Entrada Prohibida,* and worked his way forward and upward, finally reaching the captain's quarters. He knocked, heard a grunt, entered, and then waited, watching the captain's bent head with wary interest. He had seen the master only flittingly during these first twenty-four hours.

For a considerable time the captain sat coldly staring at the mass of papers spread on his desk. Finally he transferred the stare to the doctor and said, "Yes? Dr.—ah—Swend-strom?"

"I am disturbed, sir, by the condition of the woman in Forty-two."

"Really?" The captain arched his fine-drawn eyebrows, so making his face a mask of tired, delicate sarcasm. The captain looked like a slightly rundown Conrad Viedt, but he had the instincts of the parts portrayed by Eric von Stroheim. Brutality filtered through shopworn elegance was amazingly effective in causing his subordinates, and often his passengers, to experience the sensation that they were cloddish idiots. As the doctor quailed slightly beneath the eyebrows' indication that he was an ass, the captain said, "I'm disturbed by several things, rather more important than one female. And an American, at that. We are a day late." The imputation was clear enough: doctors had been a large source of his troubles in the first two weeks of the current voyage. "Is she going to die?"

"No. But—"

"Then don't disturb me with the problem."

"Eventually"—the doctor looked far younger than his papers stated and seemed even younger than that as he hesitated; then he went on, obviously nerving himself to a necessity—"eventually we—I, that is, but I as a member of your staff—may have to account for her condition. And the fact that we sailed despite—"

"We were already under power when she fell. It says so in the log. Logs do not lie. 'Account for her condition?' So? She has a broken arm, no?"

"Yes, and probably a slight concussion—"

"And a few bruises on her shins and chin. So? They assured me from Hamburg you were a good doctor. You cannot set a broken arm? No?" The effort of speaking sustained English, which he spoke well but irritatedly, was telling on him, and as usual instead of turning red with anger he was turning white.

The doctor said hastily, "She also suffers from amnesia, it begins to seem. And hallucinations."

"Ah?" The captain brushed his finger across his long straight nose as if he were disaccommodating a fly. "So, she is crazy? So, maybe she was crazy before she came aboard?"

The doctor didn't seem able to think of an answer to that one.

"The American," the captain said suddenly. "The other American—two this trip, *Grüss Gott!*—he is a doctor of the mind, no?"

"Well, no." The doctor looked uneasy. He said, "That is, surgically speaking, yes, to some degree. But—well, I didn't mean—"

"Why not? Why shouldn't you mean? It is not good for your dignity? This—consultation, you call it, no?—this is not correct?"

"Well, yes, but . . ."

"But what? You want from me some assurance that the woman will suddenly recuperate? That the log will be made to show she was crazy to begin with? That you are brilliant? Logs do not lie. If there is anything wrong with this passenger's mind and we have on board a psych—psych—"

"A neurosurgeon."

"—a whatever-he-is, and we have failed to present to him the case, then we—you—will really look funny. Call

in this doctor. Gently, he is a passenger." The words were
delivered ungently. The captain looked down at his papers.

The interview was over.

3

"Dr. Owings."

Max brought his gaze up out of the swimming pool and
saw a man in a blue uniform with a caduceus on his arm.
Max stood up, held out his hand, and said, "How do you
do?"

The ship's doctor, an astonishingly good-looking young
man, was obviously not German, but his English was so
unaccented that it was not easy to identify. One might
guess that he was Canadian.

The doctor glanced at the busy young deckhand and
then moved his handsome black eyes back to Max's face.
"My name is Swendstrom. Forgive my delay in presenting
my compliments. I've been busy."

"The woman who fell down the stairs? Serious?"

"Well, no." But the well-cut young face looked very
serious. "She sustained a broken arm, minor contusions."
He stopped.

Max said, "And?"

The doctor smiled, his teeth very white against dark
skin. "And—I don't know. Perhaps a concussion. She is not
very clear. Confused, you know? So I thought maybe, that
is, we thought, the captain and I, that since we have distinguished neurosurgeon and diagnostician aboard, he—you
—might be willing—?"

If the captain knew enough to call him "a distinguished
neurosurgeon" he knew at least part of the rest. Max felt

his temper rising, controlled it, and said with so elaborate a courtesy that his words achieved almost a burlesque of medical etiquette: "My dear Doctor, I should be delighted."

4

It was a corner room with two large portholes, but the curtains were drawn and a minute passed before Max's eyes accustomed themselves to the dimness. He saw first, because she stood up, the plump, elderly stewardess, and then, as he found the figure in the corner bed, Max felt an instant surprise. The face and shoulders were wrapped like a mummy's, like the invisible man's. The rest of the body was heavily blanketed. He said, "A few contusions? I had not realized the bruising was so extensive."

"Oh, entirely minor," Swendstrom said, "but, as you see, extensive."

"Yes." The mummy's eyes were open but as Max moved forward until he was within their range the eyes did not follow his motion. He leaned over until he had attracted their attention, but they still moved slowly and without interest. He said, "My name is Owings. Dr. Owings. Are you comfortable?"

She didn't answer. The eyes were blank, the pupils dilated. He said, "Morphine?"

From behind him the doctor said, "Atropine."

Max said, "Um," and to the patient, "Hello. My name is Dr. Owings. What's your name?"

There was still no answer, but from behind him Swendstrom said, "Elizabeth Smith."

Then the woman spoke. "That's what he says." Her high voice was toneless, but it contrived to register timid disagreement.

"He's mistaken? Well, what is your name?"

"I don't know." The words came slowly.

"Well, then, if the doctor says—"

She spoke more quickly then, and the timidity was very noticeable: "I'm afraid of him."

Now, that was unusual. The young man was movie-star handsome. Besides, victims of brain injury, like those who suffered from less tangible psychoses, were inclined to put more trust in their would-be healers than in anyone else. Naturally. Max turned and looked inquiringly at Swendstrom, who spread his hands and shrugged. He said, "It makes things difficult. I think I remind her of someone."

"No. It's him I'm afraid of. He hurt me."

The young man repeated the business of spreading his hands, and Max nodded. Setting of the arm, unguents for the bruises and cuts, all could have been painful. To a dislocated, shocked mind the pain could have connected itself to the agent, the doctor. But it was nevertheless unusual. He said to Swendstrom, "Amnesia? Other indications? Chronic, possibly?"

"How could I know? I never saw her before." He looked flushed, even angry. Max wondered why. Did he wish to be thought of as medically proficient, too proficient for this minor setback, this distrust on the part of a patient?

Max turned back to the figure in the bed. "Are you comfortable?"

"No."

"Something hurts? What hurts? Let's see if we can fix it."

"*He* hurts. His *being* here hurts." She emphasized by loudness. A monotone was not uncommon in such cases, but this voice was unusually high-pitched.

Max turned to the young man and shrugged. Swendstrom hesitated, then backed up a step or two. He finally said grudgingly, "I'll be in my office, Doctor," and turned and marched out.

The woman sighed. Looking down into the dull eyes, Max could discern a dim relief. They were dark eyes, very large. The eyeball itself, neither flat nor deepset, was large, and so was the iris. "Now," he said, "Tell me where you hurt?"

"He stuck a needle in me. I don't have much pain. Arm aches a little. That's all. Somebody pushed me, you know."

"You think so?"

"I know it."

"Then you remember it?"

Hesitation. "No. No, I don't remember it."

"What do you remember?"

"I don't know what you mean."

"Where does your memory stop? Do you remember getting on the boat?"

"Boat?" She struggled slightly beneath the blankets, then subsided. "My God, am I on a boat?"

"That answers my question, doesn't it? Yes, we're on a ship."

Surprisingly, the woman showed a flash of humor. "Shanghaied," the high voice said.

It was a hopeful flash. Max played to it: "Too many movies," he said. "This is a very pleasant, first-class passenger ship. Isn't it, Stewardess?"

The elderly woman in white said gutturally, "A beautiful ship we have."

"Yes," Max said, "murals in the dining room, excellent food, cozy bar. No figures skulking about. Called the *Tilburg*." He waited, but there was no flicker. He said, "Not the sort of ship onto which one gets shanghaied. Not"—he smiled, and as always his was a very engaging smile—"not Maugham."

The eyes brightened fractionally. She asked, "And where is it going?"

"Lots of places. Port Saïd, Djibouti, Colombo, Penang, Singapore, Hong Kong—ending in Japan. I'll ask what your destination is."

"Heaven is my destination." The voice was dry. "Colombo, Singapore—not Maugham, huh?"

Max laughed. "That round goes to you. Now try to tell

me where your memory stops." He realized she was re-
taining consciousness only with great effort, and in view of
her timidity it was a brave effort. He said, "Quickly, please.
You're getting sleepy."

"Yes." The eyes blinked and opened wide, but they were
dimming. "I don't remember anything."

"Not London?"

"I've never been in London."

"Then you do know where you have been?"

"I know where I haven't been." That was almost tart.

"Agreed. And where you have been?"

She hesitated. "America?"

"Well, of course. You're American, after all."

"*I* know that."

"So you do know some things, you see."

"And you're American, too."

"And you recognize accents. So you do have some memory."

"*If* that's memory, Doctor."

She had him there. It was not memory, of course; it was
mere recognition. Recognition without recall. Paramnesia.
But paramnesia could be a perfectly normal phenomenon,
and so it proved nothing, for good or evil. Well, she had
humor, despite her fright. He could put that to use. The
fright itself was to be expected in such cases, but from all
the signs he suspected that she was normally a retiring,
easily frightened, docile sort of personality, which still did
not rule out intelligence. He could play on the humor and
the intelligence and on the fact that she seemed comfortable
with him. He took a step toward reinforcing that embryonic confidence: "We are the only Americans on the ship,
I think. You and I."

"So we have that in common, too."

"Too?"

"Neither of us likes *him*."

"My dear lady—" He stopped.

"That was wrong of me?"

"Well, mistaken. I thought he was good-looking, pleasant, young, and—I'll be unprofessional, if you like—inexperienced. That's all."

"I'm going to sleep. . . . So psychoanalysts are honest?"

"More than most people, probably. But I'm not a psychoanalyst."

"No?" It was a mere murmur now.

"I'm a surgeon, a specialist in brain surgery, spinal surgery, such things. My name is Owings."

"Mm?" The eyes had closed.

Max felt foolish, and the emotion was becoming much too usual. If she hadn't recognized her own name and was sure she had never been in London, how in hell could he expect her to recognize *his* name? He had better stop this nonsense before it achieved the status of a psychosis.

He looked speculatively at the sleeping figure; it told him nothing. The curve of the cheek, as it started downward below the dark eyelashes, suggested she might not be very old. The figure was so heavily bundled that all he could tell was that she was short. He reached under the blanket and withdrew the nearer arm, the right arm. It was not bandaged, so the left arm must be the broken one. Then he sat, looking down at the hand that lay limply in his own.

It was not noticeably very young, nor in the least old. But it was, in an undefinable way, an unusual hand—both capable and artistic, sturdy and delicate. It did not fit the voice or the personality. But the normal personality was obscured, of course.

He shrugged, put the hand gently beneath the blanket, nodded at the stewardess, and went in search of Dr. Swendstrom.

5

The doctor's office, far below decks, was small and windowless but neat and well-equipped. All was surgical white and metallically disinfectable. Swendstrom, behind a small desk, seemed to have regained poise and confidence. He said, "Well, Doctor?"

Max shook his head. "No beginnings of a diagnosis. I'll examine her. I will say—and even this much is foolish before examination—that the case seems a bit peculiar."

Swendstrom raised heavy, perfectly arched black eyebrows.

"Well, a blank period is usual in cases of accident, when people sustain a blow on the head. But retrograde amnesia of that type usually covers a brief period, say the ten minutes before the blow. Fifteen minutes. Psychologists suggest that it merely proves that learning takes a little time to be absorbed, and that what the person who has been banged on the noodle has forgotten was merely not yet absorbed. Total amnesia, on the other hand, is usually the result of a traumatic experience, a neurotic anxiety—an intense form of repression. The person is suffering from an endopsychic conflict. In consequence one has a case like this, in which the patient forgets everything, except, usually, how to talk, eat, and manage the facts of life. And they often remember historical facts, and such things. As this woman seems to behave. She recognized a reference to Somerset Maugham, for instance."

"But now you're saying she's a usual case. I thought you said it seemed unusual."

"Well, this is an accident case, but she's behaving like

someone in the grip of a severe anticathexis, someone suffering from an acute, unresolved conflict."

"Oh. I see. What does it mean, then?"

"It *could* mean that she was ripe for some sort of breakdown and the accident triggered it. I'll examine her—get my case."

"I'll take care of a few things and join you there."

Max would have been perfectly happy without the young man's "assistance," but it wouldn't do to say so.

Max's cabin was on A Deck, the same deck as the woman's, but on the opposite, the port side.

His cabin door wouldn't open.

Max tried again. He hadn't locked it, which didn't change the fact that it was now locked. The button that would call the steward was inside, naturally. He looked up and down the narrow passageway, but a siesta solitude still ruled.

He walked down a flight to the purser's desk. No one was there either. There was a closed door behind the desk. He stepped around and knocked on it. Nothing happened for several minutes. Finally the door was opened, with noticeable reluctance, by a young man. He had blond hair, formally Nordic good looks, and one stripe on the sleeve of his unbuttoned jacket. Probably a purser's assistant and so, Max figured, probably a linguist.

He was wrong in his final assumption. The young man had several English phrases, and he most likely had got his stripe on the basis of them, but by no stretch of imagination could he be considered as English-speaking.

After minutes of getting nowhere, Max resorted to German. He could not be said to speak it, but his mind was more pertinent than the young assistant purser's. "*Der Schlüssel,*" he said. The young man made the instant assumption that Max was proficient in German and delivered several guttural questions in frighteningly rapid succession. "*Nein, nein!*" Max said painfully. "*Geben Sie mir den Zimmer-Schlüssel.*"

"Ah! You must see the steward!"

"How?"

It took a hell of a time, but Fritz, Max's cabin steward, was finally produced, looking extremely sleepy, and the door was opened. As Max stepped past him into his cabin he said, "Thank you. Don't lock the door in the future. I never like to bother with a key."

Fritz's English was excellent. He said, "I never lock a door, sir, unless I find it locked." The door closed on that, and Max stared at its inner surface. Well, he thought, the fellow was tired and disgruntled.

He and Swendstrom approached Cabin 42 at the same time from opposite ends of the corridor. Swendstrom also carried a case, a small square first-aid kit. He said, "Sorry. Got held up. You shouldn't have waited."

"I've just arrived."

"Um?" The young man opened the door and stood back for Max to precede him, and so was second into the room, but nevertheless his acknowledgment of shock came first. "My God!" he said.

They both stood rooted for a minute, peering across the dimness at the bandaged figure.

When Max had left her she had been an impeccable Invisible Woman, as white as sterilized gauze can be. Now she, the pillows, and the sheets were a bloody mess.

Someone behind them squealed, "*Gott in Himmel!*"

Max turned. It was the stewardess.

Swendstrom started by unwinding the yards of gauze. Max opened his case and held out a pair of surgical scissors. The bandages then peeled off rapidly.

The girl—she was a girl, and not to be called a woman; not, at least, in everyday terms of the English language—was unconscious and seemed, through the crusts of blood, to be peacefully unconscious.

"Crusts of blood," Max thought. She had shed enough blood to create an appearance of carnage, and yet in so brief a time the blood had flowed, ceased, and was clotted and darkening.

The phenomenon was soon explained. The dozens of cuts were of the shallowest variety. They had bled profusely for a minute or two and then nature, not greatly offended, had made the beginnings of its own repairs. When sponged clean the cuts emerged as thin slits along the hairline, beside the ear, under the chin. One crossed the jugular but had barely penetrated the epidermis. Her arms and hands, too, were cut.

As Swendstrom reached for gauze Max glanced at the stewardess and then said in a low voice, "Don't you think thin strips of plaster would do? Leave her to the air, huh?"

"You think so?" Swendstrom also glanced at the stewardess. He said stiffly, "Yes, I expect you're right. But how on earth could such cuts have reopened? After twenty-four hours? And, as you see, they were extremely shallow in the first place."

Max said, "Um. What interests me is how she sustained them."

"Oh, probably the edges of the risers as she fell. It was a hell of a fall. Didn't you see it?"

"No. You did?"

"I certainly did. A fantastic, headlong business. I thought most of the newcomers were witnesses."

"I was already in my room. In fact, I don't remember seeing her at all, not on the tender, nor on the dock while we waited to board the tender."

"No? Well, we were all pretty bundled up. I didn't notice you on the tender for that matter."

Max looked absently at the stewardess, who had been silent since the moment of her first exclamation. She was standing, rigid, hands clasped, looking down at the freshly bandaged woman. Then Max transferred his gaze to Swendstrom and said tonelessly, "You were on the tender?"

"Of course. . . . Oh, I see. You think of me as part of the ship's complement, which I suppose I am. But only since yesterday. I boarded at Southampton."

"Oh." Max fished around in his mind and then chose one of the many questions that naturally arose. "But how had the *Tilburg* come so far without a doctor? Isn't there a law? International law? Something about a ship that has over twelve passengers—something like that—being required to carry a doctor?"

"Yes, there is. But the ship's doctor died right after they left Rotterdam. Took him off in Southampton Sunday morning. I'm his replacement." He paused, then said, "Well, we're finished here." There was an unspoken question mark at the end.

"I shouldn't think so. There's the stewardess."

Swendstrom stared at him. "So what?" he said.

"Well, where was she?" Max wondered if the fact that it was undoubtedly none of his business came through too clearly. He said, "It seems to me you might ask her."

"But why? She was probably in the ladies' room."

The stewardess said, "No, sir. You called me, Doctor. Have you forgotten?"

Ah, so she did really speak and understand English. Max looked inquiringly at Swendstrom, who said, "I? No, Frau Schmidt, I did not."

She looked confused. She pointed to the telephone, almost accusingly. "It rang," she said. "Someone said I was to come to the kitchen. I thought it was you. I thought you wanted to speak to me about diet."

Max said gently, "And then?"

"Well, the kitchen was locked, and I looked for the chief steward or the chef . . ."

And it was the same story of a delaying action.

6

Clarkson, very bland in a black suit, was at the table when Max arrived for dinner. The purser appeared next in a state of such intense nervousness that he appeared to have an ague. On his heels came the Pitkethlys, he being massively solicitous, she appearing to cringe beneath his overhang like a tiny monkey beneath a descending club of gigantic proportions. And if she was nervous to begin with, the purser's jitters instantly communicated themselves to her. Max noticed that Clarkson was aware of her panic; for the first time he had something of the air of a clergyman—stern but kind.

Soup was eaten in silence. In the pause before the fish course Clarkson appeared to find conversation necessary. He addressed Max: "That poor woman who fell down the stairs. Have you seen her?"

"Have *I* seen her?" Max repeated idiotically.

"Why, yes, Doctor." Clarkson appeared to be innocently surprised. "It seems indicated. Don't tell me they have been so foolish as not to—"

"Of course. Yes, I examined her late this afternoon." Max felt stiff all over, but he was relieved to discover that his voice sounded natural. "A broken arm and minor concussion. Some abrasions. Natural with a fall."

"Did you see the fall?"

"No," Max said. "Did you?"

"No, I'd found my cabin by that time. Heard the commotion and came out too late. Missed the—" In the tiny pause Max wondered if he had been about to say "fun." "Missed the fall itself," Clarkson said blandly. "It was a bad tumble, then?"

"It was described to me as being head over heels, and the bruises—"

The purser said jerkily, "I saw it. Naturally, since I remained in the lounge until everyone was cleared. It was a—a—a very bad fall."

"Hell of a," Max thought, mentally supplying the missing English. But he could think of no way to put into English his own question: Who was near her at the time? But it was none of his business, and he certainly didn't want to initiate any alarms, even though his medical conscience was offended. That medical compulsion of his was too highly developed, he well knew—too strong, almost a fixation. But he wasn't going to permit it to force him into making a fuss. He bent to what he assumed was fish and was surprised to see chicken legs. The first bite disabused him: they were frogs' legs, giant variety. Max had a vision of the first of all the courses of his life that might have been called "pre-med": high-school Biology I, which he had been enchanted by at thirteen. But the vivisection of giant frogs was one thing, the eating another.

As his fork clattered loudly to the floor he thought of the psychoanalytic contention that droppers, breakers, and spillers were often the victims of guilt complexes.

After dinner, the passengers went up to the lounge, where coffee was served. Although some had been aboard several days, little groupings had not yet taken place. The newcomers of the previous day had added the note of completion that would eventually lead to the establishment of after-dinner cliques, which would in turn become drinking partnerships and shuffleboard foursomes. There would be the hypnotized bingo players, the snarling bridge players, the prayerful ship's-pool crowd, and the idiotic "race-horse" bettors . . . but thus far the new passengers had been weary, had retired early, the sea had been heavy, and the debut had been postponed.

Nevertheless, debut or not, opportunity or not, the oddly assorted passengers behaved with the inherent shyness of humans the world over. As they filtered into the lounge by ones and twos, they chose to sit not with the people they thought looked interesting or desirable but instead, with head-ducking speed, they sat at the closest table, at the first empty one, or in the quietest corner.

One Englishman, the only man to behave with deliberation, earned Max's respect and envy. He was an imposing type, sixty-ish, large, pompous, with a cane that probably was dictated by arthritic limbs (Max noted his gnarled hands) but seemed to suggest a war wound, and magnificent white hair that contrived to look as if it too were a badge of a war gallantly suffered through. He entered the lounge, stood motionless for a full minute while he took careful inventory, and then deliberately march-limped toward the large center table at which sat Mrs. Hausman. (Max later learned that she was always called "Madame" Hausman, but no one ever explained why the Chinese widow of a German should be so addressed.) Madame Hausman had forsaken her magnificent French and American clothes for a cheong-sam. And although her Occidental clothes had been chic and becoming, the Chinese dress, a standard model turned into an evening gown by the richness of its material, was breathtaking. The high collar added to her proud carriage, the slit skirt showed magnificent legs and showed them in the usual way, to mid-thigh.

Max, who had come up the stairs only a minute before the white-haired Englishman, had taken a hasty look at Madame Hausman—blue-black hair, blue-silver dress, and golden thigh—and at her table, stage-center of the room, and had then moved rapidly (scurried?) to his left, half-bowed to the woman sitting there, and sat promptly down (collapsed?).

Then (safe?), he stared at Chinese beauty.

"Lovely, isn't she?" said his table companion, and Max, reprimanded, dragged his eyes to the socially proper level.

But the woman's face showed no sign of reprimand, envy, or pique. She was glowing with open appreciation of Madame Hausman's beauty. When she stops glowing, Max thought, she is going to be one of the plainest women I have ever seen. If not the title holder.

"I am Miss Elkin," she said, in British.

"How do you do. Max Owings."

"How *dj'* do? Isn't Madame Hausman simply breathtaking? I do wish I were going as far as Hong Kong. I'd so like to see more of Chinese women. But I'm going only to Miri. To visit with my sister. She married an Australian, an engineer, and they live in Miri. I'll stay until the return boat of this line comes by and then go back home. That will afford me almost four weeks in Miri. I do *so* look forward."

According to Clarkson's obviously knowledgeable estimate of Miri—"a hellhole"—what was being afforded to Miss Elkin seemed hardly a matter to glow over.

Miss Elkin answered that point. "It's my first time out of England. Then I return to school."

"To—?"

"To *teach* school." Miss Elkin smiled. "I am," she added unnecessarily, "a schoolteacher."

And now, Max thought, he probably knew absolutely all there was to know about Miss Elkin.

As coffee was served them, he found he was staring no longer at Madame Hausman but at Miss Elkin. Why was she plain? he wondered. She was—fifty? An anatomist, he examined her chin: no, she was not fifty. The line of her jaw was entirely firm, and it was not of the square variety that sometimes serves to preserve the illusion of youth. Not square at all, her face was an almost perfect oval, the hairline being particularly well drawn. But the eyes were an undistinguished pale blue and the hair—thin, fine stuff, yanked severely backward into a little bun—must have started as a pale, unshining blond, and it had now, by the addition of gray strands, become dun. Miss Elkin didn't have a downright bad feature—excepting perhaps her eyebrows, which were sandy, sparse, and widespread—but she nevertheless contrived a total plainness. Or would, when she stopped glowing.

"May I," asked Miss Elkin, genteelly sipping coffee, "tell you a risqué story?"

Max choked, righted his coffee cup in time, and then murmured, "Delighted." It was probably not the perfect response, but no other had come to him. You can't judge by appearances, he said to himself for the millionth time.

"Well, a friend of my sister's once came to London and took me out to dine. *So* nice of him. *Such* a nice young man. He *did* live in Hong Kong, and he was telling me how beautiful Chinese women often are. As he was a sociologist, he was also interested in the manners and mores of the Chinese. He mentioned that Chinese women's dress modes were dictated by the shame they would feel in showing any of their neck. To say nothing of bosom. They simply cover up, practically to the ears."

"Yes," Max said, looking at the stiffened collar that touched Madame Hausman's lobes. Probably would have choked a Western woman.

"On the other hand, they have no false sense of shame about legs. There's always that high split in their skirts."

"There is, isn't there?" Max looked at the golden thigh across the room and realized that the color was not strictly Madame Hausman; her stockings were delicately threaded with gold.

"Well, the young man told me that in the streets of Hong Kong one need look only at the inclination of a man's head to discover whether he is Occidental or Oriental. All white men walk around with their eyes at thigh level, and all yellow men keep their heads high, the better to examine the white women's throats."

Max laughed. The picture itself was funny, and the comment on Man humorously wry, but his laugh was largely one of relief and gratitude as Miss Elkin reëstablished herself in character.

Miss Elkin glowed with accomplishment, and most of

the heads in the room turned. Not only was Max's rare laugh an infectious one, but the room's occupants were still in the grip of silent propriety; the genuine laugh had mildly shocked them.

Then all heads turned toward the center door, where a parade was entering.

First came the captain, impeccably got up in a starched and pleated shirt, dazzlingly white beneath an evening version of his uniform. His gold braid, of which he wore improbable quantities, was as blinding as the shirt. On his handsome but hatchet-like face there was a wide smile, and this struck Max as being impossible. If Conrad Veidt's face was not designed for wide smiles, this man's was even less so. Nevertheless, the new bits of porcelain that served the captain as teeth competed with his braid and his linen.

To his left, a proper pace to the rear, was the chief officer. He was a pleasant-looking, youngish man, who also wore a smile—a stiff and unhappy little grimace that clearly overlay a torture of apprehension. Of what? Max wondered.

Behind the chief officer were three stewards. The first bore a tray of coffee cups and saucers, the second carried brandy, but the third's function was not immediately clear, since he was empty-handed. It was explained immediately: "Music, Heinz!" the captain shouted to him. He had arrived at Madame Hausman's table. "Music!" he boomed, and beamed around the room.

The audience stirred in response, and an embryonic gaiety set in. Brandy, if thought of, had been shyly unordered, but now the room began to glow with the green of Chartreuse, the crystal clarity of Cointreau, the warmly murky darkness of Drambuie. And cognac flowed, at two marks the German variety, six marks the French.

Max offered Miss Elkin a drink. She unexpectedly accepted, then expectedly chose a crème de menthe frappé.

Music came out of the wall, bad music, with a disproportionate number of waltzes.

And the captain danced.

The captain, it was obvious, loved to dance. He danced very badly, and why he loved to dance explained itself in short order: Max was not the only anatomist in the lounge; the captain was a feeler, an in-fighter.

The captain danced first and, as all the astonished watchers were soon to realize, with comparative circumspectness, with Madame Hausman. Then he cased the room, and offered himself—hands, knees, outthrust pelvis, and all—to various of the assembled ladies. He showed no shyness in his choices; few of the middle-aged matrons among the dozen or so women were honored. Since there was a very small sprinkling of the near nubile, he danced with a very small sprinkling of the females present.

The fear that Max had felt or imagined when he first boarded was now a clear and explainable presence in the room. The women, young or old, handsome or homely, feared that they would not escape the workout. Their husbands were panicked as to what they would do if their wives were among the chosen, and how they could possibly do what they knew they would do—nothing. And the single men, like himself, were so deep in shame for their sex that they tilted over into fear of life, life that could produce this minor but disgusting bestiality with its undertone of bullying. For who could flatly refuse to dance with the captain?

His first partner, a young English girl, left the lounge immediately after her trial by hand and knee. The second, a handsome but not young Italian woman, pleaded illness in the middle of her dance. Looking at the gold cross atop her high black neckline, Max considered that the illness was probably wholly legitimate. (He later learned that she was a missionary en route to Brunei.) His third partner, the half-Malayan, half-Filipino beauty Clarkson had identified for Max—although young, although clearly the bride of the Scandinavian young man she was with—was nevertheless a match for the captain. She was a superb dancer, and she employed her ability to throw him off stride. Since he was incredibly bad to begin with she found it easy to bring him to the edge of catastrophe. Twice she stood coolly aside and waited until he dredged himself away from her and into some semblance of rhythm.

Max glanced curiously at her blond husband, and was charmed by the young man's small smile. How nice to be proudly married to so cool and competent a young woman. And then, remembering Clarkson, Max too smiled. A cool and competent young woman—not a half-Malayan, half-Filipino young woman.

Miss Elkin, probably misinterpreting Max's smile, said dubiously, "He's very *gay*, isn't he?" Max decided that she absolutely refused to believe what she was seeing. And then, as the captain returned to give Madame Hausman another twirl, Miss Elkin brightened. "But it's so good that he's so nice to Madame Hausman. That he honors her."

Max choked on brandy, and as he mopped at the table, thought, I must stop spilling, dropping, and choking. He said, "Um."

"You know the story?"

Good lord. "Um—no." A different story, please heaven?

"Well, I'm sure she must be the widow of a man who was the chief mate on this boat. He and the captain were very old friends, schoolmates, that sort of thing. In fact" —Miss Elkin blushed slightly—"they served together during the war." The blush, Max decided, was for their having been on the wrong side of the war. "And then, just about four years ago, they, this ship, had to take part in an attempted rescue. It was in the North China Sea, a very high sea at that moment. The captain sent the chief and four seamen out in a boat, and they floundered and sank before they reached the small Chinese junk that was in trouble. The junk sank at almost the same moment. They picked up no one, not the chief, not the seamen, no Chinese. I think there's little doubt that this must be that man's wife, since he was married to a Chinese. Don't you think, Doctor? Her name in the passenger list is spelled in the same way, with one 's' and one 'n.'"

"You called me by my title," Max said quietly. "Had I mentioned I was a doctor?" He hadn't tackled Clarkson, undoubtedly a worthy opponent, so why lash out at Miss Elkin?—But he mustn't lean over backward. The question was hardly "lashing out," and his reason for asking might be simply the piling up of recognition.

And then Miss Elkin's innocent surprise reminded him of Clarkson's. "Why," she said, "aren't you the same man? I thought I remembered the name, not a really usual name. About five years ago, a little more, didn't you win that prize? Not the Nobel but the other one, the diagnostic—"

"Yes," Max said hurriedly. "I did, Miss Elkin, but I wouldn't have thought that one person out of a million would remember it, if he had ever come across it in the first place. Please, how on earth did you come to know that?"

Miss Elkin blushed. "I have total recall," she said. "A memory so good it's often embarrassing. I read a great deal, every sort of thing, and I go to the cinema perhaps rather too much. And then I remember it all. As I say, sometimes it's embarrassing."

It was, to Max, simply fascinating. And it probably explained something that had momentarily puzzled him. "Then," he said, leaning forward, "the story about Madame Hausman, you read about that? Nobody had mentioned it to you?"

Miss Elkin nodded.

Ah, he had thought she wasn't the sort to pick up gossip within twenty-four hours of boarding.

"Total recall," Miss Elkin said, "and abnormally keen senses too. I see better, hear better, and have a better sense of smell . . . most confusing."

"And this memory, have you always had it?"

"As long as I can remember. And I can remember farther back than most people seem able to. I have very clear pictures of things that must have occurred when I wasn't much over a year old. But, as I said, it's actually embarrassing. For instance, did you know that there is someone

37

aboard who is, well, incognito?" Max shook his head. Royalty? he wondered in confused amusement. "Well, there is, and—"

The young doctor said, "May I join you?"

Max stood, Swendstrom sat, and close on his heels came the purser. Introductions followed, and Miss Elkin became the only woman in the room who had three men to herself. Good for Miss Elkin, Max thought, and noted that she was slightly flustered. He suspected it was Swendstrom's startlingly good looks that brought it on rather than the number of her escort. Miss Elkin was entirely human and entirely feminine, he thought, but a superior breed of her sex, nevertheless.

The purser said, "Has he been at it already?" He was looking at the captain's table, and Max realized that the music had stopped some time ago.

"Yes, do tell me," Swendstrom said. "All I've been hearing is of the captain's terpsichorean feats."

Max said, "The captain has been dancing."

"Ja," the purser said, "I am very sure of it. If one can call it dancing." Forget Swendstrom, who had just boarded, Max thought; the purser was a member of the ship's usual complement. Did ships' crews and officers talk openly in front of passengers about the master? "It drives poor Mr. Haas crazy," the purser added.

Max looked confused and Miss Elkin murmured, "The chief mate." She had been reading the passenger booklet, Max realized, and total recall had set in. He smiled his thanks. He said, "Now I know why the young chief looked so—ah, apprehensive."

"Ja," said the purser. "It makes him uncomfortable and he doesn't understand. There are more people around here who don't seem to understand." He turned in his seat and inspected Swendstrom angrily. "Don't understand anything!"

Swendstrom looked thoroughly taken aback, and the purser immediately reverted to sadness and fear.

Max wanted no fusses, however incidental. He poured oil: "Would you like some brandy?"

Swendstrom nodded, but the purser said, "I rarely drink."

"Coffee?"

"*Ja*. Thank you."

The music started and the captain leaped nimbly to his feet. He bowed gallantly over a German woman, youngish but not as young as the captain seemed to prefer. Also, she had the face of a gay horse. Max was momentarily puzzled by the choice but as the young woman stood up the captain's reasons became clear. She had an opulent but superb figure, Germanically full but thin wherever possible.

A slow waltz gave the captain a chance to roll with the ship, and, to the embarrassment of everyone in the lounge, his partner was obviously his soul mate. She gave as good as she got.

The chief looked agonized, the purser looked gloomily into his coffee, Miss Elkin looked incredulous, Swendstrom combined astonishment with amusement. Max wondered how he himself looked.

Clarkson said in his ear, "You look nauseated."

Introductions were made. Miss Elkin had four men.

Swendstrom said, "Will you dance, Miss Elkin?"

Max, who had thought his face was at least as inexpressive as the next man's, began to have doubts about that as the purser explained, "The captain demands that the officers dance. 'Be social,' he says, but I think he looks for a screen, a smoke screen, one says. I shall get up in a minute, may *Gott* help me. Who, please tell me, who shall I choose? Who looks kind? I am a man of lead on a dance floor."

"The bride of the Scandinavian," Clarkson said. "She is superb, and you will suddenly think you are superb. You will dance lightly all through the voyage."

The purser seemed even sadder. "A fantastic thought, Mr. Clarkson."

Clarkson nodded soberly. "The light fantastic."

The purser looked puzzled, then abandoned puzzlement for the greater torture. He sighed, stood, and approached the handsome young woman.

"So you've been around here all along?" Max asked Clarkson.

"Because I saw the bride's ordeal? Yes, I was standing in the corner back there, sighing for the souls of men."

"So you do occasionally think of men's souls?"

Clarkson's pink face split into an infectious smile. "Now, now, Doctor. You imply that I think too much of the human body? I consider that impossible because I do not make a distinction. Until the afterlife, I consider the two indivisible. Therefore I do not believe in original sin. Or perhaps I have my horse and cart tumbled, perhaps it is *because* I do not believe in original sin that I consider the soul and body indivisible while they are on the earth."

Really? Max thought. It sounded like hash. What did come through to him was that Clarkson seemed more and more unusual as a man of cloth. Max (who did not believe in original sin either) had thought that particular acceptance was de rigueur for clergymen.

Clarkson said softly, his face as good-natured as usual but without its habitual smile, "In simpler words, Dr. Owings, I believe that God put man on earth for the prime purpose of procreation. The prime *temporal* purpose, that is. Being the All-Knowing, He naturally gave humans the necessary equipment and, equally important, the necessary desire. But, in the way that He made all men imperfect, because perfection isn't human, He permitted the logical flaw: sometimes they couple without procreating. This is not to make them hateful, is it?"

"No," Max said. "I am a doctor. My understanding is of the body."

"The body? Or the mind?"

Max considered that, and then his own relieving smile broke through. "I make no distinction. I consider the two indivisible."

Clarkson did not smile. "I agree," he said. He seemed to dismiss the matter. He said, "Look at the purser."

"Not leaden. But very rickety. All those long bones."

"But he looks less unhappy than usual, don't y' think?"

"I do. And you were right in your choice of his partner. One can almost think he is a dancer. But the person to look at is Miss Elkin."

"I have." Clarkson nodded, and the two were silent as they watched Miss Elkin and the young doctor.

Swendstrom, despite the fact that the name indicated Scandinavian origin, both looked and danced like a Latin. "Swendstrom has curlicues," Max commented.

"As in fancy penmanship." Clarkson nodded again. "But she *is* surprising, isn't she?"

She was more than surprising, she was superb. Miss Elkin danced fully as well as the bride who was the purser's partner, and Swendstrom's curlicues gave her a chance to display her grace. It could not, Max thought, be a result of practice. Neither was it a matter of having attended dancing classes.

"Unself-conscious," Clarkson said.

"And yet she's shy."

"Not the same thing."

That was true, of course. Besides, Miss Elkin had a very nice figure. It was as contained as she herself was, as understated as she was, but everything was in proper proportion and nicely shaped.

"I used to enjoy dancing," said the surprising Mr. Clarkson.

"Really?"

"And I danced well, if I do say so."

"Then why not do the captain a favor and join his officers in providing a smoke screen?" Max nodded toward Mr. Haas, who was struggling with a large English matron.

"I have not danced since my wife died."

What did one say? "Ah," said Max.

"Twelve years."

"That's too bad. A tropical disease?"

"Childbirth."

"Ah. And the child—?"

"She is twelve. A very nice girl. I called her Mary."

"Um. Well, if it was a first child—"

"First child!" Clarkson turned his round face to Max to afford the full effect of his astonishment. "Haven't you listened to me at all, Doctor? Mary was the eleventh of our children. The oldest is thirty-eight. He is a doctor, like yourself. Another boy teaches economics in London University. One is a sheep farmer. One is a clergyman, a bit stuffy for my tastes, however. Five are married, and the rest are still at home with me in Miri, when they are not in school."

A half-hour later, as he went down the winding stairs toward his cabin, Max made sober note of three things:

It was all very nice for Miss Elkin to explain that she remembered his name because of the medical award he had received some five years before, but if she read so voraciously and remembered so completely she undoubtedly knew of his later and larger share of publicity—and notoriety. The latter, unlike the Franklin Award, had even been accompanied by a photograph. The notoriety had been confined to England, but she was English and had just come from there.

Second, if she ever stopped glowing she would undoubtedly be hopelessly plain, but *did* she ever stop glowing?

And third, the tread edge of each of the stairs he was descending from the lounge to his cabin deck—and Elizabeth Smith's—was rubber-tipped.

WEDNESDAY

SCHIFF *Tilburg*
SHIP

Mittwoch den *16* ten *Januar*
Wednesday the   of *January*

41°17'N Breite und *09°28'W* Länge
Latitude and   Longitude

Tages-Distanz: *377*   Seemeilen
Day's run: Nautical miles

Zurückgelegte Gesamtdistanz bis heute: *667*
Total distance covered up to today:

Restdistanz bis: *Genua*   *7303*
Distance still to be covered to:

The dancer of the night before had disappeared without leaving a trace. In his place was the captain, cold, cruel, ascetic. The gleam of his braid was still high, even in the pallid light of the dull morning, but it got no competition from his teeth, all tautly invisible.

"Yes?" the captain said. Then, as visions of the home office and the hand manual for passenger-ship captains danced almost visibly through his head, he modified the greeting: "Yes, Herr Doktor?"

"I've come to report on the condition of the woman in Cabin Forty-two."

"You have? Why?"

The answer to that question was interesting but it was an answer that Max was certainly not going to give to the captain. The truth was that he had no wish, and had had no intention, of going anywhere near the captain. Max's usual painstaking attention to medical propriety was heavily muffled by his new sense of caution, his reawakened desire to create no ripples, and certainly to cause no tidal waves.

But the elderly stewardess had taken the matter out of his hands.

He had dropped around early in the morning, nodded at the old lady in white, and glanced down at the patient. He said, "Sleeping peacefully, um? Well, sleep is a great healer. I'll come by later."

He nodded again and started for the door, but before he reached it, the stewardess said, "You will see the captain, Doctor?"

Max turned. "See the captain?"

"Why, yes, sir. You will report to him, will you not? As I—suppose—Dr. Swendstrom will also." She paused and said, "I too must go to him later to ask that my duties be rearranged."

"I see," Max said, and nodded ambiguously.

Back in his room, Max had given the matter thought. Did the captain direct the arrangement or rearrangement of a stewardess' duties? Was the old lady threatening him? And if so, why? He decided that she had taken a dislike, or perhaps just a distrust, to Swendstrom (intelligently

44

enough, since Swendstrom was so patently unprofessional) and she merely wished to see the proper thing done.

For reporting to the captain *was* the proper thing to do, and the more Max thought about it the more it became the unavoidable thing to do.

And that was what he replied to the captain: "It is proper, I should think, to report to you on the woman's condition."

"You think I have not had a report? From my own doctor?"

"I have not given that any thought whatever," Max said untruthfully, "but I don't see that it affects the matter. I thought, at the least as a courtesy, I should come directly to you."

"With what? Are you not able to fix the woman?"

To himself, Max said, Hold your temper! To the captain, "Help her to recapture memory? I don't know yet." Into the teeth of the captain's rudely obvious skepticism, Max flung a few more words: "I was talking about the criminal attack."

The captain put the thin black cigar he had been holding in an ash tray and leaned back in his chair. He said, "The woman *fell* down the stairs. The log says so. Will you please to explain just what is criminal about that?"

So Swendstrom hadn't reported. Or had he? Max said, "I am talking about the attack of yesterday."

"This business of 'reopened wounds'? Sheer nonsense."

"Your ship's doctor and I agree that the wounds were fresh."

"I disagree."

"My goodness, Captain, I am a physician. I am stating a medical fact."

"A very inexact science. No latitudes, as it were. No longitudes. I consider that you are mistaken. But mistaken or not, there is little sense in worrying the matter. I presume you are capable of patching these openings?"

45

"The young doctor attended to that. But I am speaking—"

"You suggest the doctor is not capable?"

"I most certainly suggest nothing of the kind, and I can't imagine why you think I do."

"The 'young' doctor—"

"A statement of fact. I had no intention of being patronizing."

"—is thirty-nine. Even to me, at fifty-seven, thirty-nine does not seem pathetically young."

Max said, "Oh. I had misjudged his age."

"One should not make hasty judgments. You yourself should know that well, since you look nowhere near your forty-eight years. Well, now, Dr. Swendstrom has bandaged these minor reopenings, and that is that."

It was a long time since anyone had tried to dismiss Max as if he were a schoolboy. Trouble or not . . . He said, "Not in a legal sense."

"You are a lawyer as well as a doctor?" The sarcasm, like the man, was a whiplash.

Clenching his teeth, and every reflex that led to hitting out, Max reflected that doctors meet very little discourtesy in their day-to-day life. Nurses and internes are practically servile, patients are at the best grateful, at the least they are tactful, feeling themselves to be at the life-and-death mercy of the physician. And the rest of the world pays varying degrees of courtesy to the title of doctor. Therefore, he said to himself, I am probably merely unaccustomed to such rudeness and I must suppress both my ridiculous temper and my most unprofessional desire to kick his teeth in. He said, "As a doctor, I am required to report criminal attacks to the authorities."

Probably the captain was even less accustomed to contradiction than was Max to discourtesy. And almost as incapable of subduing anger. At any rate, he was turning white, which, in Max's experience, often signaled the onslaught of temper in a violent-tempered individual. He picked up his cigar and leaned forward slightly. He said,

"Ah, I see. You felt you had to report to the authorities. Well, you have now done your duty." He waited for Max to rise.

And Max was stopped. It was true: the captain represented authority. So Max had done his duty and could now relax. But a devil-take-the-consequences anger had a firm grip on him. "Well, then, I can take it that you will report the matter?"

"To whom?"

"I am not, as you implied, a lawyer. I am assuredly not a marine lawyer. I presume you'll report to the German authorities, to the authorities in the nearest port, or—"

"Genua?" the captain asked with a rising inflection. "You suggest I invite the *Italians* aboard my ship to 'investigate' something?" His horror was palpable, and Max felt that he was viewing a rare moment of simple honesty on the part of the captain.

"Perhaps not Genoa. Perhaps not the Italians. I haven't the slightest idea to whom a matter of criminal attack should be reported, but I presume you *do* know, and I am asking for reassurance."

"Be reassured." The captain put the long cigar in his mouth and contrived to remain ascetic despite it and more distinguished because of it. "My conclusions will go into the log." He picked up a fountain pen and bent his head over the papers on his desk. "I am extremely busy. The log will show what I feel it should show. This business of 're-opening'—well, I shall think about it. Good day."

Max looked at the long, thin white mouth, so tightly closed, and got up and left the room.

Outside he paused and took a deep breath. Then, as a dog with water, he almost literally shook off fury. An underlying cold anger remained, but the desire to hit out had fortunately left him. Anyway, he reflected, remembering the captain's shiny smile of the evening before, knocking the captain's plates out would hardly be much of a feat.

Well, he hadn't wanted to, hadn't intended to, but somehow or other he had managed to do his duty: The captain

47

undeniably represented authority. The matter would probably end there, and that was just as well.

Max shook his head and started down the corridor. Swendstrom had discussed 'reopened wounds'; so had the captain. Therefore Swendstrom had reported to the captain. But Max had never used the phrase. The wounds had not 'reopened'; they were newly etched the afternoon before. That would have been his certain opinion even if the right hand that had lain so limply in his early on the day before had not been entirely unscarred until this afternoon, when it had developed a razor crease across its back.

2

In London, early on that Wednesday morning in the middle of January, the sun made not even a feeble attempt to come out. It was a damp, cold, gray day, and Detective-Inspector Medford's light gray eyes were equally bleak as he waited in the superintendent's anteroom at a little before nine.

Early morning interviews with the superintendent, Medford had learned from long experience, were inclined to be even less comfortable than usual. As the superintendent was inexplicably fond of saying of himself, he was "not a particularly reasonable man." He *was* a man who wanted results. Offered a report, he was given to saying, "I'd rather have a solution." And, solutions aside, even the report that was all Medford could present at this moment was a recital of frustration.

But the interview started out with unprecedented mildness. The superintendent seemed thoughtful, a most unusual mood for him. His words were as expected, but his tone moderate: "This is the third day since the Harley Street affair?"

Since it was not yet nine o'clock, that didn't seem a fair way to phrase it. "Yes, sir," Medford said.

"And the fifth since the murder actually took place. According to the doctors."

"Quite." Doctors! Medford thought with a touch of bitterness.

Surprisingly, the superintendent said, "Doctors." But he seemed ruminative rather than bitter. He added, "What have you got?"

Medford considered briefly and decided on simple honesty: "Almost nothing," he said flatly.

And still the superintendent didn't blow up. "Give me the facts, then."

"Yes, sir. The body of Dr. Clarence Barkland was discovered in his Harley Street consulting rooms by the charwoman at seven in the morning on Monday, January fourteenth. Day before yesterday. He had been shot twice, at close range, by a twenty-two caliber pistol. Gun is there, no bullets left, and it belonged to the doctor. But there is no possibility of suicide. Forgetting the two bullets, the angle of—"

"No possibility of suicide. Accepted. Carry on."

"Yes. Well, the smallness of the bullets, according to Laboratory's scientific officer and the doctor, was outweighed by the point-blank range. He probably died instantly, and he probably died on the previous Saturday, the twelfth. The doctors are not prepared to narrow it much farther than that, due to the coldness of the apartments. His consulting rooms were not his home—he was a bachelor and had a service flat in Green Street—and he did not usually accept appointments on Saturday or, of course, Sunday. That accounts for a number of things—among them, why the office was so cold and why his body was not discovered sooner.

"The place showed no sign of a struggle. The murderer left nothing behind. No one was noticed entering, not even the doctor himself. No one was noticed leaving. No one was noticed, period. It is, of course, a quiet neighborhood, especially on a week end."

"And the doctor himself?"

I'm coming to it, I'm coming to it, Medford thought with some irritation. He said, "The doctor was a psychoanalyst. He was apparently much sought after, and much respected by his confrères, of whom I have interviewed a number." Doctors! he thought again. He said, "They are a—well, a cagey lot, rather. Full of 'ethics,' which seems to mean that they stick together like a guildhall of Musketeers. It was several hours before I learned that Dr. Barkland had been involved in the Terrence Clinic affair. That was ten years ago, and—"

"The abortionist ring. Yes, I remember. Then how come he still had a license to practice?"

"Three of them did retain their licenses. Eleven were tried, on different counts. That is, they were accused of varying degrees of involvement and/or complicity. One was a medical student, three were internes, and seven were practicing physicians. Eight served prison sentences, up to seven years apiece, and three, all qualified physicians, got off. Those three had been enlisted, were undoubtedly on the verge of guilt, but the Crown was unable to prove that they had actually performed any of the illegal operations. Barkland was one of those three, all of whom got off with a severe reprimand.—That is a very sketchy outline. I got it from Billings, who helped to uncover the affair. I have sent for a complete file."

"I see. Well, carry on."

"There is no immediate reason to think that the Terrence Clinic connection has any pertinence. But it is there in the background."

The superintendent nodded. One had to know as much as possible and try to ignore the unnecessary.

"Dr. Barkland's appointment book is missing. At first I thought that would mean little; we would simply check with his nurse. But psychoanalysts seem to manage their practices rather differently from other physicians. Dr. Barkland did not have a nurse in his office. Nor a secretary. Not exactly."

"I find that astonishing," the superintendent said, and added, with a flash of his usual ascerbity, "And especially astonishing is your phraseology—'Not exactly.' "

"Quite," Medford said tiredly. He had been up late, studying Dr. Barkland's files, a most unrewarding and rather exhausting pastime. He said, "It appears not to be too astonishing that he did not have a nurse, or a receptionist, or a regular secretary. His practice and habits made such an employee basically unnecessary. He kept his own appointment book and he kept his own records—'case histories,' I suppose one would call them. Also he kept the inner door of his two-room suite locked, and the outer door, the one that opened onto the public corridor, unlocked. In that way he was not disturbed while with a patient. The next appointment let himself in, and then waited for the inner door to open. No need for a receptionist in that respect. He did have a part-time shorthand-typist. A Mrs. Doris Sweet, a medical secretary turned housewife, came by twice a week, on Tuesdays and Thursdays. On those two days the doctor started his afternoon appointments an hour later than usual. Mrs. Sweet arrived at one and left at three. The doctor had a sandwich before she arrived, she made him tea, and then he dictated, largely correspondence. She typed it and left. On rare occasions he dictated some medical notes, some details of those case histories, but that was out of the ordinary. He kept the data in a sort of shorthand of his own devising—a personal method of writing quickly while someone was talking to him. The files in the inner office are all in that odd little script. It is not immediately decipherable."

"Code department?"

"Well, I have no doubt but that they can untangle his system—I don't suppose he intended long-term secrecy, if he intended secrecy at all—and I suppose thoroughness indicates that I must put them to the job, but it seems a bit of a waste because Mrs. Sweet is positive that a good portion of the files are missing—she is judging by the look of the drawers, which seem merely half as full as usual to her —and common sense indicates that the one or the group of interest to us is among those missing . . . At any rate, I was explaining that Mrs. Sweet can be of little value because the doctor did not often have her type the notes. She makes the point that he did not feel it was worth while taking up the time—not her time, but his, because, you see, she could not read his shorthand. He would have had to dictate them."

"How about a list? His patients, their addresses. Didn't he have a file-card system of some sort?"

"No. He was apparently the rare man who reduces red tape. On the face of each folder in the large file cabinets, there is noted, in his minute handwriting but not in code, the name, address, dates of appointments, age of the patient, and similar data. Each file a nutshell."

"Um. What about the correspondence? Didn't she keep carbons?"

"Yes, but doctors don't seem to write to their patients. They write to other doctors, they write to their Aunt Mary, they write to their landlord to complain about the drains, they write to medical journals to take issue, they pay bills to their clubs, and to the telephone company. So forth."

The superintendent regarded the ceiling. Then he said, "You are looking for a patient?"

"In view of the fact that you, sir, are not the press, I will say yes. I have nothing concrete, but the missing files and missing book hint strongly at murder by a patient. Besides which, they are most likely a group of not too well-balanced people. Not outright insane, although that can't be ruled out either, but on the face of it, not entirely level-headed. It seems to me that the case, offering no clues at all, offers two hints: One, a patient. Two, the doctor's record of involvement in that shabby abortion affair. That opens the possibility of blackmail."

"He hadn't changed his name by deed poll?"

Medford shook his head.

"So the secret was not a secret. It was an open fact."

"Yes, but—usable, I think."

"Perhaps, perhaps. Yes." The superintendent sat forward in his chair. "Well, I have another theory. Not a theory, a— You know about this morning's development?"

Development? "While I was waiting to see you Sergeant Robb mentioned that a body had been fished out of the Thames this morning at six. Lower Thames? That what you mean?"

"Yes. Which gives me two murders in less than a week and two of the kind the newspapers like best, God help me." He wasted two seconds on self-pity; then he said, "I put Trehane on it. I didn't know at first— Well, let me give you what we have got: Body is totally unidentifiable. Something in the water had been at him. No face left. Not much else, either. Apparently throttled. He has yet to be postmortemed, of course. After the P.M. the lab will get him and they can go to work on an index finger that seems to have a pad left, but they haven't got much hope. And suppose they succeed in getting a print? This isn't the States with their comprehensive files. Sometimes I wish . . ." The blasphemy of wishing that England be in any way like the States apparently overcame him; he abandoned the thought right there. "All they have been able to tell us so far is that he was about five feet eight inches tall, fair-complexioned, with large bones for his size and superbly healthy teeth. Big progress, what? But"—he paused weightily—"in the inside pocket of the shreds of his overcoat there was a stethoscope."

Medford was not fascinated. He said, "Yes?"

"Well," the superintendent said, with something resembling embarrassment, "that proves nothing at all, of course, certainly not that the man was a physician, although I feel that it indicates the possibility." Obviousness momentarily overwhelmed him, and then he went doggedly on. "But it adds to something else and gives me a—a—" He broke off, and then continued, pushing out the words as if each were a dray horse: "Yesterday evening I was given the responsibility, in so far as we have a responsibility, for a new case, quite a—a peculiar one. This, mind you, is still *another* case, a third one."

The superintendent was not only embarrassed, which was unprecedented, but he seemed confused. Confusion was as uncharacteristic of the man as embarrassment. When confusion assumed elephantine proportions, as it quite often did in their hide-and-seek world, the superintendent had a unique ability to face the great gray hide—and simply ignore it. He then followed up by demanding results. But now . . . Medford said gently, "Yes?"

"Yes. Ah, it seems a man died on a German ship shortly after the ship pulled out of Rotterdam, outward bound. That was the evening of the twelfth. Last Saturday night. She arrived in England the next day, on the thirteenth, did not sail the same day, as scheduled, but waited over until Monday. Meanwhile the Southampton authorities were asked to take over the body. It seems to have been assumed by everyone aboard that he died a natural death, of food poisoning. But Southampton's routine autopsy revealed that he had been poisoned. Not by food, that is. Here"— he fished among his papers and came up with one that he handed across his desk to Medford—"is the autopsy report."

"Quite," Medford said, dropping the paper in his lap and wondering what he was supposed to do with it. But he was apparently expected to do something, so he offered a mild thought: "If it is a passenger-cargo ship, it most likely carries a doctor. He's the one who should have—"

"The dead man was the ship's doctor."

"Oh?" Medford chose his words carefully, "And there is a link?"

"Look, Richard, I'm being, ah— I feel somehow that there are just too many doctors around. Mostly dead. There's also one alive. On board this ship."

"And that's surprising? You mean it's odd that they replaced the dead doctor?"

"No, no. Of course they replaced him. At the first port of call. Which was here, England, that is. That was one reason for the day's delay—to sign on a new doctor. Put an English doctor on as a temporary measure. But there is another doctor aboard, a passenger. Dr. Maxwell Owings."

"Oh." Medford nodded. "Well, he was en route to some biggish job in Hong Kong, wasn't he? Wasn't that supposed to be one of his reasons for haste and perfidy?"

"According to the Fleet Street Flash."

The superintendent's use of the nickname amused Medford, although he wasn't sure why it should. Lady Flasley, who had inherited her chain of newspapers from her father, had also inherited his nose for tasteless, senseless, and occasionally criminal sensationalism; she was invariably called the "Fleet Street Flash," on the Street and off, but the nickname seemed to Medford to come oddly from the lips of his superior. Medford said, "So this Dr. Owings had his day in the journalistic glare. Makes me feel sorry for him, but—"

"She might have had something this once."

"I think, sir, that it's that kind of thinking that keeps her going. 'Where there's smoke there's fire,' et cetera."

The superintendent exhibited an unusual note of self-defense: "Well, he didn't sue. A medical man, and of his standing. Why didn't he sue?"

"American," Medford said. "That's a total explanation. They don't have our taste for the national sport of libel and slander suits."

"Well." The superintendent looked dubious. "Then why didn't he at least explain? He didn't offer an explanation."

"That simply shows how much good an explanation does. The Flash didn't print his explanation. The *Times*, the *Guardian*, the *Morning Telegraph* and one or two others did—and rather mysterious reading it made, too, if

55

you don't happen to be a follower of the Flash's muddy sheets. Since the others had never mentioned Lady Flasley's homemade 'news,' the doctor's comments read very mysteriously. You were on holiday, sir?"

The superintendent nodded, accepting the offer of an excuse; after all he *had* been on holiday. "And what did the doctor produce as an explanation?"

"In about eighteen understated, gentlemanly, professional words, he said almost nothing at all. But it somehow seemed exactly the right thing to do."

The superintendent still looked dubious. "Well, I'll agree that this American doctor's neglect—reported neglect—of a dying child can't have much to do with this rash of dead doctors but . . ." He paused, and then said with an effect of stubbornness, "I am not given to whims." Nothing could be truer, Medford thought. "That's *your* specialty." Not quite true, Medford thought. "But I simply have a feeling that there are too many doctors around."

"I understand that sort of feeling."

"But you don't share it?"

"Well, this is all new to me. No. At least, not yet."

"Um. Nevertheless, I'm going to send you."

"Send me?"

"Oh, didn't I explain? Well, the international complications have been infinitely intricate. That, thank God, is none of our affair. Outcome is, however. The West German, Dutch, and English governments have decided that there must be an investigation into the death of this ship's doctor, and the job has fallen to us. I should imagine we were asked because we did the autopsy and we are nearest to the ship." The growing expression of dubiety blanketed his face. "Although it seems to me to make little difference where one flies from, and it also seems to me that I have enough dead doctors. Still, the thing is in my lap. So. You will please turn over, temporarily, the Barkland investigation to Trehane. That is, the two of you are to work together. Consult with him about his corpse-with-stethoscope and give him your data on Barkland. And then you will

56

fly to Genoa, arriving there Saturday. You will board the German ship *Tilburg*, which is expected to arrive early on the afternoon of that day. The ship's captain is being notified to expect you. Get all the details from Robb." Sergeant Robb was the superintendent's secretary. "They sail on Monday. Please try to tie the matter up by that time."

Medford felt stunned and feared he showed it. "Genoa. Tie the— You mean the murder of the ship's doctor? *Was* he murdered?" He looked blankly down at the autopsy report. "Or the possible connection of these medical men? Or—" He stopped. Or what? His normally almost silver eyes looked smoky.

"Richard, I don't quite know what I mean. See what you can see. Use that, um, intuition of yours, which I'll admit I usually deplore. And if you need more time, well, sail with the ship. Its next port of call is Port Saïd, due to arrive there on the twenty-fifth."

"Port Saïd," Medford said numbly. He passed a hand over his cap of blue-black hair. "Yes, sir."

3

Max looked at the face that the captain had reported as belonging to a thirty-nine-year-old. There wasn't a wrinkle on Swendstrom's clear olive skin, not the slightest sign of sag. He looked in the neighborhood of thirty. Max said, "You got the passport for me? Good." He held his hand across the doctor's small desk. After a second, Swendstrom put the small Copenhagen-blue booklet into it. Now, why was he reluctant about it? Max wondered.

"Bring it back, will you? Request of the purser, who apparently hasn't finished his homework." Swendstrom paused. Then he said, "You're going on with the case?"

Max stared at him. He said, "Well, of course. The girl can't simply be left in that amnesiac state."

"No, no, of course not. I meant . . . You haven't been to see the captain?"

"I did that little thing. I gather you also saw him. An experience, huh?"

"My God." Swendstrom smiled. Max looked at his teeth, strong, very white against the olive skin, and even. Even? They looked absolutely perfect. What had Clarkson said, on rather a different subject? ". . . He made all men imperfect, because perfection isn't human." Well, that didn't apply to this man's teeth. Like the captain's? No, he could see the gums; the teeth were not false. And then Max had the answer: Swendstrom's teeth were capped. He added the fact to another that had been impinging on his nostrils: the man either burned incense, used cologne, or else a musk deer had been loose in the small office.

Swendstrom said, "He lectured me on medicine. Perfect nonsense, every word he said, but I found I wasn't doing much contradicting. The fellow freezes me clear to the marrow."

"He is definitely chilling," Max said, "but that can make no difference to the treatment of a patient."

"Of course not," Swendstrom agreed hastily. "Certainly not."

Max sat in Elizabeth Smith's cabin looking down at the small blue booklet, and was reminded of the captain: "You look nowhere near your forty-eight years," the captain had said. True enough, but it underlined the fact that all passports had been collected, and they had not been returned.

Max brought himself to the matter at hand. "Your passport says you are twenty-six," he said to the girl. "Last November seventeenth."

"And my name is Elizabeth Smith."

"Betty?"

"Rings no bell." Her deep voice rose slightly, "But if it's Lizzy I prefer to remain anonymous."

Max smiled. Swendstrom, so advised, had discontinued sedation although he had shown his usual and incomprehensible reluctance. Max had pointed out that the scratches were merely that, the arm was a simple break, and there was nothing else wrong with the girl. "Except amnesia," he added, "and my desire is to make her less foggy, not more so." And so today she was clear-minded. The concussion had been very slight. She was also unchaperoned, the stewardess having been allowed to return to her normal duties. He said to the girl, "I just don't see you as a Lizzy."

"But you do see me? I am here?"

What kind of a quirk was that? "Certainly," Max said quietly. "You are very much here."

"Don't be alarmed, doctor. I merely mean that, if only as a female, it's pleasant to know that someone can see me. I can't see myself."

Max waited.

"No mirror." She had an impish grin. She added, "I know, I know—I'm not supposed to get up. But however rocky I was yesterday I can walk perfectly steadily today, even in competition with this tub we're in. And so I can see no reason to have the old stewardess carry a toothbrush to me when I can go to it. But . . . did you ever research the fact that people look in the mirror when they brush their teeth? I can't see why it's necessary but I found that my teeth didn't feel clean when scrubbed in secret, so to speak."

Her teeth were white, not so startlingly so as Swendstrom's, but then, unlike his, hers were natural and her skin was very fair, providing less contrast. In her, contrast lay between eyes and hair, both very dark brown, and the fair skin. She was, in a way, very pretty, with the prettiness of a child. Her nose was a button, her mouth small and sweet, and the darkness of her hair naturally extended to her eyelashes, which made her large eyes look bigger than they

59

were, gave her that look of children whose faces have not
yet grown up to match their eyes.

—And that estimate was purely a first impression, Max
decided. For the small face had character, the deep voice
was adult, the personality had force and charm and a sort
of bravery.

"Still, secretly done or not, I prefer to brush my teeth
over a basin rather than over a bed. And I can't see why I
shouldn't walk, despite the handsome young man's instructions." She made a little face, a wrinkling of the nose.

"Why the face?"

"The young doctor."

"You're still afraid of him?"

"Afraid?" She looked surprised and then thoughtful.
"Well, I certainly don't think so. Let's say I'm not charmed
by him. I'm simply more—more comfortable when he goes
away. Did I say I was afraid of him? Back there when I
was cock-eyed?"

"You suggested it."

"What do you know?" She pondered it. "Well, I wasn't
all there, I suppose." She grinned, and the grin contrived
to be both impish and sad. "Nor am I now, huh? But the
doctor is gentle and kind and he seems really concerned
about me, so it doesn't make good sense not to like him,
does it?"

"Perhaps he reminds you of someone?"

"Perhaps." She nodded slowly. "That might be it."

"I'm sure he'd be willing to have you walk now."

"I can get up? Right now?"

"Yes. You have a robe?"

"The stewardess found one. It's on the inside of the bathroom door."

The dressing gown was red plaid flannel, rather like a
schoolgirl's. Max took a linen towel off the rack and
glanced at the wall over the sink: no mirror. As he returned
he pushed the steward's bell outside the bathroom door.
He draped the towel around her arm, tied it behind her

neck, and said, "For the moment. We'll fix up a better sling later. Will you be able to manage?"

"Never use my left hand anyway."

He looked at her quickly.

"Oh," she said. "Well, I *know* I am right-handed."

"Um. Well." He handed her the flannel robe and said, "I'll wait outside."

The steward was the same one who served Max's cabin. Max said, "Ah, Fritz. Will you please bring a mirror for the bathroom wall?"

"But there is a mirror. Over the sink. In every room, sir."

"Not in Cabin Forty-two."

The steward hesitated. He said, "Are you—"

"Positive," Max said. "No mirror."

"Well, but there are no extra mirrors. That is . . . Just a minute, please." He moved to the far end of the corridor, opened an unnumbered door, and reappeared in less than a minute carrying a wood-framed mirror, about eighteen inches by twenty-four. Max recognized it as being the same as the one in his own cabin. The steward said, "A mistake. Please to excuse it. I suddenly remembered having noticed it in the linen room."

Max knocked on the door, and the girl opened it. She was very small.

The steward started in but Max said, "No, I'll hang it. Thank you."

"Please," said the steward, in direct translation. He stared at Miss Smith and then departed.

Max carried the mirror to a porthole. He said, "An error, the steward explained. Here you are."

The girl came toward him slowly, then took the mirror and looked at her face by the gray light of the day. She said, "Not very distinguished."

"Not bad."

"No?" She looked again, and then handed him the mirror. She said, "I don't remember that face. It looks familiar in a way I can't explain, but I don't really remember it."

"Don't worry about it for a while."

"The scratches aren't bad, are they?"

"Not at all. They'll disappear without a trace in a day or so."

"Even the ones beneath the plaster strips?"

"They're no worse than the few you can see. In fact, if you ask Dr. Swendstrom he'll probably take off those strips."

"They're funny scars, aren't they?"

"You fell down the stairs, you know."

"Yes." The wide eyes examined him for a minute, then she smiled. "Tell you one thing—the face needs make-up."

"And then it'll be very pretty. You have make-up?"

"There's a small kit." She nodded toward the three pieces of luggage in the corner, the topmost of which did look like a make-up case. "And oddly enough, I'm sure I'll know just what to put on and how."

"Not so odd. Quite usual. Now, let's sit down."

They sat facing each other across the small round table in the room's center. Max opened the passport he had left there. "Here's how you look with make-up. Theoretically. Passport pictures are not known for being very good likenesses."

She looked. "I suppose it's the same face as the one in the mirror, but the one in the mirror looks more familiar."

"Understandable. What else does this tell us? Um. Not much." He noted an admission in the passport but decided against mentioning it. "You entered England a little over three months ago. London Airport. And this triangular one tells us what we know, that you left via Southampton on January fourteenth, two days ago."

"I *don't* know England." Then she dropped the air of defiance and shivered. "January," she said.

"Yes. And those two are the only stamps in the book." He turned back to page two. "The passport was issued on September twenty-second of last year and it wasn't a renewal, so you took it out in order to make the trip to England." He turned the page. "Issued in New York City. Unfortunately these new passports don't mention professions so we'll get no clue from that."

"Professions?" Her eyes widened. "You mean I might *be* something?"

"You might indeed. Perhaps a doctor like me."

"Oh, I don't think so. I don't *feel* like anything." She grinned. "Nothing very important." She held out her hand. "May I see?"

He gave her the blue booklet and she examined it soberly. " 'Height five feet two and a half inches, hair brown, eyes brown, wife x x x, minors x x x,' and signature undistinguished. Undistinguished, of an undistinguished name. Do you suppose all those x's mean I'm not married and have no children?"

"No, merely that no one is traveling on your passport except yourself."

"I don't *feel* married." She saw his expression and smiled. "I seem to keep repeating what I am not. If you can understand that sentence."

"The sentence and the emotion. Negatives are usual in such matters. But nothing seems actively familiar?"

"No, but there's one other negative, one other thing I don't feel—I don't think I know New York." She grinned again. "I don't *feel* like a New Yorker, and it's my impression that that is usually a very active feeling."

Max spent the next fifteen minutes in aimless conversation, establishing a rapport, hoping for a sign. He got none, but when he rose to leave she permitted him to get almost to the door before she said, "Doctor."

"Yes?"

"That mirror. I also had two mirrors of my own. One was in a powder compact in my purse, the other in the top of that make-up case."

He said quickly, "How do you know?"

She shook her head. "No, I don't remember them. But there are marks, bits of dried black adhesive where mirrors had been." She waited a minute, her large eyes very dark but very clear, and then, when Max said nothing, she added, "I suppose they could have been broken or removed long ago?" The deep, musical voice was dubious.

"Perhaps," Max said.

He stared out of his porthole at the unending sea, at the queasy-making gray swells, and saw the dark eyes of Elizabeth Smith, filled with question marks. He found that he agreed with her—it seemed unlikely that all mirrors would disappear by accident or coincidence. But why remove them? Amnesia-by-accident is not inducible.

On the other hand . . .

He opened the passport that lay on his lap. The inside cover, under a boldly printed "Important" said, "This passport is NOT VALID until signed BY THE BEARER on page two." She had indeed signed it on page two, in a rolling schoolgirl's hand. However, the paragraph beneath the word "Important" read on: "Please fill in names and addresses below." And "below" there was room for the Bearer's address in the United States, a Foreign Address, and an Address to be Notified in Case of Death or Accident. All three were blank. That did not invalidate the passport; all the government had said was "Please . . ."

But why had Elizabeth Smith not responded to that request? Just such an accident as the booklet tried to provide for had apparently happened to her. Another coincidence?

Max shook his head.

THURSDAY

SCHIFF _Tilburg_
SHIP

Donnerstag den _17_ ten _Januar_
Thursday the of _January_

_36° 13' N_ Breite und _06° 41' W_ Länge
Latitude and Longitude

Tages-Distanz: _387_ Seemeilen
Day's run: Nautical miles

Zurückgelegte Gesamtdistanz bis heute: _1054_
Total distance covered up to today:

Restdistanz bis: _Genua_ _916_
Distance still to be covered to:

Thursday morning the sun made an attempt to come out.
It was a feeble stab, but the passengers responded like a
medieval bride to the first small smile of a stern husband.

People appeared at breakfast in the dining room.

Shuffleboard was played.

Children gaily threw the deck-tennis quoits overboard. (From the resigned expression on the deck steward's face Max surmised that the loss was overdue.)

A few ladies donned shorts. (A hardy sex, Max thought. In heavy slacks and a turtlenecked sweater, he was none too warm.)

Max sat beside the empty, netted pool and tried to view the passing scene with peaceful detachment, but he wasn't permitted the luxury. A superb figure, very partially clothed in tiny white shorts that revealed two halves of golden-apple buttocks, and an equally diminutive shirt, which impartially revealed two halves of golden-apple breasts, loped up to him. Over the figure there loomed a horselike face.

"I," said the horse's mouth, "am Fräulein Gotthelf. Good morning!"

Max stood up. "Max Owings. How do you do?"

"Oh, I know *your* name, Doctor!"

Max felt no touch of sensitiveness. This was flirtation, not recognition. But a simpering horse was an unnerving sight. "Ah," said Max. Her perfume was overpowering.

"You did not come to the lounge last night." It was an accusation.

"I went to bed early. Was there dancing?"

Miss Gotthelf thrust out her lower lip. A sulking horse was no less strength-sapping than a simpering one . . . I've got to stop the comparison, Max thought. Miss Gotthelf said, "Well, yes. But not really. The captain didn't come either. There were *no* attractive men. Not really. If you see what I mean?"

He couldn't say yes. Could he say no? "Um," said Max.

"*Guten Morgen, Fräulein,*" Mr. Clarkson said. "Dr. Owings. You looked very gay last night, Fräulein Gotthelf. I thought the chief danced well, didn't you? And in view of it all you look very bright this morning. Very bright." Mr. Clarkson's pink leer was much more pronounced than usual. He sniffed luxuriously. "You smell, too," he added.

"Hee-haw," said Fräulein Gotthelf, and cantered away.

"Was that a rescue?" Max asked.

"Was it unwelcome? I saw you looking into the swimming pool's net and its resemblance to a giant spider's web came forcibly upon me. Was I wrong?"

"You ask the damndest questions. If I say you were wrong I become a predatory, tasteless oaf. But if I admit you were right I achieve the distinction of a housefly. Besides, that lady reminds me more of a horse than a spider."

"Making you a horsefly. Much more virile than a housefly."

Max laughed. "In view of your jacket, Mr. Clarkson, you are in no position to cast stones. That material was certainly not spun by any spider, but it *might* have come off a horse."

Mr. Clarkson looked down at his jacket, a giant plaid executed in a remarkably hairy tweed. He said complacently, "Charming, eh?"

"Well, it certainly brightens the day."

"Thank you." He looked highly dignified, and then abandoned dignity for a smirk. "The lady didn't need brightening, did you notice? And she had a strenuous night."

"She said there was very little dancing."

"I wasn't referring to dancing. She did a bit of it, mainly with the chief engineer, and then she retired with him."

Max looked at the pink face; the double meaning was broadly intentional, and the face radiated the good nature of a top banana. Max said, "You, my dear Clarkson, are an inveterate gossip."

Clarkson said piously, "I do not deny a deep interest in my fellow man."

"And woman."

"The same thing, and, thank the Lord, not the same thing. And speaking of which . . ." He stood up, and Max followed suit. Miss Elkin said, "Oh, do sit down,

67

please. Do. Isn't it a bit cold?" She was looking at the rotating rear of the Gotthelf, and her expression, Max thought almost tenderly, was truly lovely: Miss Elkin's face portrayed confusion, admiration, mild horror, and a large question mark. It was the first such mélange in Max's experience.

"Too cold. But you," Mr. Clarkson said, "look very charming." The tenderness Max felt was clear in Clarkson's voice. He is perceptive, Max thought, and (performing the switch that Clarkson seemed invariably to produce in him) probably a very good man.

"Well, now, *thank* you!" Miss Elkin's shyness caused her to turn rosy; her natural unself-consciousness caused her to enjoy the compliment. She glowed brighter.

Miss Elkin wore a blue wool pleated skirt. It was made of some stretchy material that Max could not identify, but the result—the stitched top of the swirling short skirt hugged her graceful hips tightly—was very pleasant. Over it she wore a loose, long-sleeved blue sweater, edged with white at the neck and cuffs. In a way, the looseness of the sweater did more to reveal her bosom than the Gotthelf's nudeness. And the blue lent color to her eyes. "I came to ask a favor," Miss Elkin said. She lifted her hand, displaying a box camera. "*May* I take your pictures?"

"Adore it," Clarkson said promptly. "I am—what are the Americans reported to say?—Ah, yes, I am a sucker for having my picture taken. I always develop as distinguished, clerical, the acme of propriety, the very—"

"Not with your mouth open," Max said. "Pose, instead of talking. Where do you want him, Miss Elkin?"

"You, *too*, Doctor. By the rail, I *think*. Don't you?"

"But unlike Mr. Clarkson, I am *not* a sucker for having my picture taken."

"The railing will be very nautical," Clarkson said. "Very appropriate.—I don't have to pose, Owings. I was born posing. And you too had better shut your mouth and be snapped.—Now, my dear Miss Elkin, I must refuse to offer my image except on a condition: when you have immortalized Owings and me—together and individually, I suggest—you must allow us to capture your charming person."

"Oh, *would* you? I want to remember this trip, y'know. It's all . . ." She paused and for the first time since Max set eyes on her, the glow diminished and threatened to fade entirely. Then she smiled and said, "Thank you. I asked the purser and the doctor if I could take *their* pictures, and then I thought perhaps they would . . . But they were—busy."

For "busy," Max thought, read "angry."

"I stole one shot, but then they rushed away," she said in sad conclusion.

"Not us," Clarkson said. "For us not the affairs of a little ship but immortalization on the Ship of Life. Now, Owings . . ."

Clarkson became the director. It was, Max realized, more than a joke; he was evidently a keen photographer. When all possible shots had been directed and snapped, Miss Elkin departed. Both men tried to keep her with them but she was anxious to take pictures of everyone and everything. So, Max thought, she could remember the trip, which would be all she would have.

Clarkson said, with no twinkle, "A perfectly charming woman. Reminds me of someone."

"Of all the nice and pathetic spinsters in the world, I suppose."

"No. Not a bit of it. She is far more than that."

"Well, I didn't mean—"

"Of course not. And I didn't mean to make you seem unperceptive. But if Miss Elkin is pathetic I prefer not to recognize it. *She* doesn't think she is pathetic, and if one takes people at their own estimates, one doesn't do half badly."

It was a philosophy Max was not familiar with. He said dubiously, "So the Gotthelf is a seductress?"

"Well, isn't she? Would you care to join me in getting up a pool on how many seductions she achieves before Japan?"

Max laughed. He said, "Forgive me, but at this moment you look positively satyrlike."

"Ah, not me, Owings. Not the conclusion one might draw. The Gotthelf may have 'em all—except me. I am a continent man."

Which, Max thought, accounted for his excessively incontinent conversation.

"Exactly," Clarkson said, disconcertingly. "May I," he continued, "speaking of continence, speaking of photography, speaking of the charming Miss Elkin, and without any excuse really—may I bore you with some snaps?"

"A pleasure."

And so Max was introduced to the Clarkson family—handsome sons, pretty girls, and a beautiful wife. Max commented on the late Mrs. Clarkson's beauty.

"Ah," Clarkson said thoughtfully. "Thank you. But honesty compels me to disagree. As the word 'beautiful' is used by this world, she was not. But she was inwardly beautiful. It is odd indeed that the camera, which is said not to lie, always caught that out. Do you suppose the truth of the camera might be a truth of God? No, that's too far-fetched, isn't it? But the camera never failed to bring out the beauty that lay within my wife—that inward glow."

2

Medford's information on the death of the doctor aboard the ship (which turned out to be the M. S. *Tilburg*, Hamburg to Tokyo and return) was contained in the autopsy report and its three appendages. The autopsy report provided a rather revolting description of the dead doctor, exteriorly and interiorly, and ended with the statement that he had died of poisoning as a result of a large dosage of a widely used antiseptic and preservative, which it named.

And who said it was murder? Medford asked himself. And answered, Nobody. The superintendent had "been given the responsibility" for a new "case." He had transferred that responsibility to Medford with instructions that Medford "investigate the matter."

So—Medford sighed and ran his hand over his black hair—he didn't even know whether he was investigating a murder or an accidental death (unlikely in view of the stuff's taste; it would need disguising) or a suicide. He moved wearily on to the first appendage, two sheets of official report from the Southampton police.

Southampton had gone through the same problem of definitions. At great length, unlike the lady behind the bolted door, they didn't say "yes" and they didn't say "no." Ultimately, after a large expenditure of four-syllable words, they termed the death "possibly suspicious." They produced one actual fact: In addition to the poison the doctor was chock full of alcohol.

The third exhibit was a group of highly official-looking governmental papers, complete with translations. It made a mishmash. Rotterdam bowed graciously out. They felt *sure* the death had not occurred in Dutch waters. (Relief sighed through the typewritten formalities.) Germany was concerned. England was consulted. England was requested. England acquiesced. (Why do we have such a damn conscience? Medford asked himself.) Italy's "cooperation" (read "permission") was requested. Italy acquiesced. (The tone here was even more pompous and far more reluctant. Medford felt that Italy suffered from a suspicion that it was being slighted. Probably they felt they should have been asked to investigate. Medford agreed heartily.

The final exhibit was a fleshless and bloodless biography

of the doctor, written on the paper of the shipping company and signed by its secretary, one Kurt Von Winckel. The doctor was named Otto Ulmann. He had taken his medical degree in the University of Würzburg in 1938; he was forty-nine at the time of death; he was married to Elsa May Gröschel in 1943; he was childless; he had been employed by the shipping line for three years and five months . . . et cetera, Medford said to himself. Despite the attached snapshot, Dr. Ulmann did not emerge at all, but remained a featureless, middle-class, middle-aged man. Medford wondered if Herr Von Winckel had ever met him.

He sighed again and looked at the clock. Almost noon. He still had to consult Trehane, but he would do it in the afternoon. First he would check through the old records on the Terrence Clinic affair, that record of the abortion ring of ten years past. Then he could turn the records over to Trehane that afternoon. He slid deeper behind his desk and opened the voluminous file.

The Terrence Clinic affair had its fascinations, mostly of diversity. One medical student, three internes, seven doctors. The punishments meted out were (as Medford had mentioned to the superintendent) widely divergent. Four of the doctors were general practitioners; the others practiced or were training toward widely diversified specialties. (The press-given title—"The Terrence Clinic Affair" —had stuck, but it was in a way misleading. The doctors had convened and performed their illegal operations at The Terrence Clinic, but they had been recruited from private practice, from hospitals, from other clinics.) The men's birth years spanned from 1899 to 1930. The majority were English, naturally, but two were Scotch, one was Canadian, and one was a New Yorker. Their names, too, were diverse, indicating that their forebears had come from widely separated parts of the world (most unusual in England). There was a Latinish name, two vaguely Scandinavian names, one Germanic . . .

All most unusual.

Medford read quickly but committed to memory the names and all the facts.

Medford was tall; Trehane was taller. Medford was unobtrusively well-tailored; Trehane was so unobtrusive that he became almost blatant. Medford's simplicity and British reticence were natural, despite his Italian grandmother; Trehane's *aire* was consciously adopted. Nevertheless, Trehane's manner was usually effective and its loss was consequently shocking. And, to Medford, funny.

"He only goes loopy about once a year," Trehane said wildly, "so why does he always have to choose me for his outlet?"

"He doesn't." Medford smiled. "He chooses me."

"You! Oh, just because you're getting an all-expenses-paid free look at Italy? But—"

"A look at Genoa, Trehane. From airport to wharf."

"But *I'm* getting your corpse, and I've already *got* a corpse. Mine is about as anonymous as a corpse can get, and that's pretty anonymous. Shoes gone, so no bootmaker check. Label yanked out of shirt, suit, and overcoat—Incidentally, that confounds me; why not strip the corpse?"

"Perhaps the murderer was solicitous. Afraid the chap would get cold. The Thames in January—"

"Now don't *you* get funny! The super is funny enough!"

For all his elegant appearance, for all his surface wit, Trehane was an extremely dogmatic man. His methods of investigation were, in so far as regulations and systems permitted individuality, as unlike Medford's as possible. Trehane operated on a basis of thoroughness: do everything, do it properly, follow up, check. If he had ever had a moment of intuition, he had slept it off. He was, in fact, a model of the type of detective to whom the superintendent paid lip-service approval. And so it was surprising that the superintendent did not value Trehane very highly, that Trehane was scared to death of him, and that (although Medford had never suspected it for a moment) the superintendent had far more faith in Medford.

After an interview with the superintendent, Trehane was always a bit confused. At the moment, he was even having trouble holding to his natural thoroughness. He said, "Please don't interrupt. You're worse than the super. What was I saying? What was I *thinking?*—Oh, yes, I had a serious point in this business of making the corpse hard to identify. The murderer throttled this chap, carefully removed all labels, papers, and so forth—and forgot a stethoscope? Yes?"

"You think it's a deliberate false lead?"

"I dunno. I dunno nothing, as your Sergeant Brooks once said to me. He was theoretically speaking of himself, but he damn well meant me. And if he said it now he'd be right. I dunno nothing, except that that stethoscope smells fishy to me."

"Well, if it's been in the water for a few days—"

"You stop it, Richard. This one is not funny. And now I'm getting yours, and that doesn't sound very amusing either."

"And I'm getting an international one, which is unhumorous from at least a dozen other aspects. I suspect that my authority is questionable—"

"Why? If the Dutch and the Germans have turned it over to us, what's questionable about it?"

"I suspect the Italians aren't happy."

"Oh. But doesn't a ship carry the law of its flag?"

"Look, Trehane, I'm not an international lawyer, which is one of my complaints, but the answer to that seems pretty clear: Not when it's in port."

"Well, then, just stay mum until you're en route to Port Saïd."

"Which only proves you've never been in Port Saïd. Otherwise you'd know that my whole idea is to keep the hell out of there. Now, look, let's get down to it."

"How can we? What have we got to get down to? Even the p.m. is taking a lifetime."

"Now, now, Trehane. Let's discuss the old man's notion seriously, and operate on the assumption that there is a

74

connection. It is undeniably true that we have two dead doctors, and a third corpse with a stethoscope in its pocket."

"One is a ship's doctor, a German, and he died at sea. The second is a psychoanalyst, an Englishman, and he died in Harley Street. (Incidentally, they seem to have met geographically suitable ends, didn't they?) And the third one could be anything, including a candlestick-maker. Also, according to this brain storm of the super's, we have a neurosurgeon, an American, that bastard Owings."

"I see no connection there, and I question that he is a bastard."

"He was considered one of the few men alive who could have helped that child, and he refused."

"According to the Flash. Hardly my idea of a dependable testimonial to character, good or bad. Still, operating on the assumption that the old man's notion has pertinence, I agree that he is one more doctor and the bouillon is getting muddy. Getting down to it, I'll brief you thoroughly on the Harley Street affair, you do the same for me, and then in Italy if I can find a trace of a connection I'll telegraph."

"Why not phone?"

"Ship to shore? I'll probably want more privacy than that. We'll see. Now, at your end, for a starter, I'd suggest a rundown on what happened to each of the eleven Terrence Clinic gentlemen, connected or otherwise. Or to ten of them, since Barkland's end is noted and entered. And throw in Maxwell Owings, as a bow to the super's notions."

Trehane looked bitterly unhappy. He was a past master with such assignments, but eleven dossiers would be a bit much.

3

Max knocked on the door of Cabin 42. After a long pause the oddly high monotone said, "Come in." The two words contrived to convey hesitancy.

Miss Smith was dressed in a dark-green wool dress with a high collar. It, like the flannel housecoat, was schoolgirl-ish. It suited her. The bandages were gone and, except for the sling, she looked healthy and pretty. She also looked scared to death. Her eyes were so widely held that white showed around them. The effect was slightly funny, like the emoting of the days of silent films. But Max knew instantly that there was nothing funny in the room.

He said, "Good morning."

"Good morning." Her face remained frozen.

He said gently, "Is there something wrong?"

"Wrong? I don't know. I'm just frightened, I think. It's —it's not nice not to know who you are."

"You are Elizabeth Smith."

"Yes. But I can't go out."

"You can't—Why can't you go out? Don't you feel well?"

"I think I feel well. But I can't go out. Dr. Swendstrom said no." The high voice quavered.

"Oh, the doctor was here."

"Yes. He took off the bandages. See?"

Her fright was so palpable that Max almost shared it. He said, "Did it hurt?"

"Well—no. But—" She paused, struggled for words, and then said, "Doctor, will you forgive me now? Just—forgive me? Come back a little later, perhaps?"

"Certainly," Max said instantly. "Certainly. See you later."

Max found Clarkson on the aft deck, introducing a group of tots to the science of shuffleboard. Two were Chinese, two were Occidental, one was unidentifiable. "No, no, Maria," Clarkson was saying to a towheaded six-year-old as Max came up, "you've got to put a bit of dash behind it, y'know."

The child replied in a series of sing-song syllables, and then looked confused. Max said, "May I interrupt?"

"Ah." Clarkson mopped his pink face. "You are extraordinarily welcome."

"I thought maybe you'd join me in a drink before lunch?"

"Delighted. Simply delighted."

He relinquished his paddle to the unidentifiable, a little boy who grasped it eagerly. Clarkson then took Max urgently by the arm.

As they moved away, Max said, "What was that little girl speaking? Sounded like Japanese."

"It was Japanese."

"Her parents haven't taught her their own language? German, I should think?"

"German. I questioned that too, and her mother looked despairing. They live in Japan and the children, three of them, go to an English school, where they naturally speak English. They speak German to their parents. They speak Korean to their nurse, who came with them when their father was transferred from Korea, and intermittently Korean and Japanese to each other. They never get confused on those four levels, but the necessity to speak to strangers bewilders them entirely. That kid spoke all four languages to me, and never the same twice in succession."

"I should imagine they'll grow out of it without difficulty."

"Oh, yes. But what was really amusing was a fifth language which I caught her using with her younger brother.

They apparently didn't like the older Chinese, and Maria said, 'Upstairs head him nobody.' To which her brother replied, 'No me say so. Me say him half head.'"

Max laughed.

"Pidgin," Clarkson said. "This the bar?"

"Yes."

The bar was small, cool, intimate, all a bar should be. It was early and the room was empty. The bartender, a small dark German, had the lonesome, efficient look of so many bartenders.

Max said, "What will you have?"

"Well, I don't drink, you know. A choice of nothings is difficult."

The bartender said, "Orange juice, sir? Lemonade. Coca-Cola. Sinalco. Tomato juice."

"Tomato juice. Wonderful idea."

"Gin and tonic for me."

While they waited, Max asked idly, "You never drink?"

"No. My excuse is that I'm too volatile already. Liquor might blow me up. Truth is that in the little things I'm very well behaved. If I were a cliché-user I'd probably say that I have no minor vices, but I'm not a cliché-user, thank God, and anyway I'm rank with minor vices. Gossiping, for instance, as you so justly pointed out.—What's on your mind, Owings?"

Max looked up, startled. "What made you ask?"

"My dear Doctor, you are mildly transparent. Introspective, sensitive, studious, highly perceptive—and the minute you stop being all of that you look like a thin brown bird dog."

"And I thought I looked mysterious! Ah, well. Since you admit to the vice of gossip, I'll admit to the vice of curiosity—"

"Almost the same thing, and both necessary to growth and intelligence. Certainly so in our professions."

"—and we can feed each other. It's the purser who's on my mind. And also the captain. You said you had sailed on this ship before, and with many of the same crew. Was the purser always so frightened?"

"Ah." Clarkson accepted his tomato juice, nodded thanks to the bartender, and took a thoughtful sip. He belatedly said, "Cheers."

"Cheers."

"I must admit, Owings, that I asked exactly the same question of myself. And the answer was, No. Unhappy, he always was. But mutedly. As if it were simply a character trait. Now he looks unhappy as if he were pursued by demons." He waited while the bartender picked up some lemons and returned to the far end of the bar. Then he said, "Purser's name is Ernst Herbst. Dreadful alliteration, isn't it? 'Herbst' means autumn, and a suitable name it is for a sere and decaying man. Not an interesting man, by no means an unusual one, but highly representative of a large group of his fellow nationals. He once told me, in a burst of pride, his history: as a youth, one of the Hitler-*jugend*; at twenty-four a corporal in the German army; by nineteen forty-five he had achieved glorious sergeant-hood. And having divulged that much, he remembered what came afterward and got scared." Clarkson looked into his tomato juice and repeated, " 'Scared.' Also typical. He respects authority and is scared of everything that might cause him to deviate from obedience. I'll make a guess, Owings. I'll guess that his present state of fright springs from some schism between the gods that rule him. Perhaps the captain is taking one line, the home office another— something like that." Clarkson sipped. "What made you ask?"

"That business of his not being willing to have his picture taken."

Clarkson looked puzzled, then startled, and finally amused. He laughed and turned a deeper pink. "Oh, you *are* priceless. Have you decided that he's 'wanted,' hah?"

Max said, with some stiffness, "It's not unheard of."

"But the doctor also refused, and the doctor is simply

beautiful, which makes his refusal even more mysterious. Are you suggesting mass crime, or a mass of criminals?"

"Ah, well." Max shrugged. "It was a thought. Silly, perhaps. . . . And the captain, was he always so, um, gruff?"

"Ah." Clarkson turned serious. "Gruff? He's abominable in a dozen ways, isn't he? However, 'gruff' is exactly what he always was, but not vicious, as he now seems to be. I'm not speaking about the ladies—he was phenomenally . . . shall we say 'forward'? . . . when I last sailed with him some six or seven years ago and he was no more than fifty then. That somewhat disposes of the 'old goat' theory, doesn't it? He was undoubtedly a young goat, he was, by my witness, a middle-aged goat, and he'll die an old goat. But his disposition is certainly far worse. However, I think there's no mystery about the causes. He had a chief mate, who was also his best friend. Hausman was one of those sweet, lovable men who are born once in a very long while. Very much a man, a hard worker, but his greatest quality was his sweetness—a wonderful man, it seemed to me, admittedly on short acquaintance, but from the way he was admired—loved—by his men . . . Well, the captain loved him too. Or so it seemed. They had served together during the war, and I think they had also gone to school together. Hausman served as liaison between captain and crew. And then Hausman was lost. There was a rescue attempt—"

"I know the story. Was the loss deliberate on the captain's part?"

Clarkson looked shocked. "Oh, I say, I shouldn't think so. That would be a harsh judgment on a fellow man, even one such as the captain. Besides—no, I shouldn't think so. He loved Hausman, you know."

"And did he also love Hausman's wife at that time?"

"Hah." Clarkson looked sternly into his tomato juice. "I don't know. I'd rather think not. But his disposition today can probably be largely accounted for by the fact that your suspicion is shared by the complement of this ship, and perhaps, according to a surprisingly outspoken conversation I had with the chief steward last evening, perhaps it is also shared by the home office. Practically everybody aboard this ship remembers Hausman, and reveres the memory. The new hands are infected by the old ones, and so they all hate the captain—for the loss of Hausman, whether it was his fault or not, for his, ah, seduction of Hausman's widow, and for his frigid superiority. Doesn't make his disposition any better, of course. They're very outspoken about their feelings, too."

"That was one of the first things that struck me. I was startled to hear officers discuss a captain in such a way, and in front of passengers."

"Shocking, yes. Makes one feel sorry for the poor devil. Incidentally, so far as Madame Hausman goes, Hausman may be better off where he is. Have you talked to her?"

"No."

"It's an experience."

"Oh? Of what sort?"

"Indescribable. You'll have to live through it yourself. Well, a footnote to all this is that the captain is like a man under sentence. Mercifully, such terms come to an end. A few more trips, and then he'll retire on a substantial pension —although I rather wonder what he'll find in civilian life. Anyway, he's riding out this storm, serving his bitter sentence in half-sobriety, and looking the other way when important trouble occurs. He chews out the men viciously for little matters, but he tackles nothing important, reports no one to the home office—probably fears they might decide against him—and, according to the present chief officer, seems to pray from moment to moment that nothing will happen. Nothing of any sort. Nothing that could be twisted and held against him."

And that was a substantial answer to the captain's reluctance to do anything about Elizabeth Smith. Max said, "So that's what the chief officer said, huh? My dear Clarkson, you do get around, don't you?"

4

This time when he knocked on the door of Cabin 42 there
was no hesitation. The "Come in" was commanding.

"Good morning," she said frostily.

"Again."

"Again?" The clear eyes seemed to fog for a minute.
Then she said frostily, "Ah, yes. The traffic is terrible
around here."

"That cliché dates you. Or rather, it is older than you
are."

"How do we know how old I am?"

"Passport."

"And who's to say it's mine? Smith. Yah."

"People *are* named Smith, you know."

"People who have amnesia? That's carrying the thing
too far."

"What are you angry about?"

"I'm not— All right, I'm angry. Wouldn't you be?"

"Having my questions answered with questions bewilders me. And that one is particularly unworkable. How do
I know if I can join you in this anger until I know what
it's about?"

"Nobody asked you to join me. Is that the famous 'trans-
ference' I've heard about? If so, keep it. And as a diagnostician are you supposed to go around being publicly bewil-
dered?"

"Who said I was a diagnostician?"

"Who's answering questions with questions?—You said
it."

"I said I was a brain surgeon."

"Well, then it was the twirp."

"The— That is not very respectful of the doctor."

"Respectful!" She achieved sincere outrage. "Why should I be 'respectful'? What on earth do I owe that—that twirp? Or is it that you feel all doctors deserve deep curtsies, pulls at the forelock? Am I supposed to pay homage, to be respectfully submissive—"

"No. Nor to be quite so redundant. May I sit down?" He had achieved his aim; a little downright fury might clear away the smoldering fumes of contained anger and permit him to try to get to basics. He said, "What are you so angry about—forgetting the, um, twirp?"

She examined him silently, and confusion flooded her eyes and overcame anger. She shifted the sling to a more comfortable position at her waist and said slowly, "Really, Doctor, that isn't very perceptive. Here I am, sitting on a boat. I am going somewhere, I don't know where. I don't know who I am. I don't know if I have a 'profession.' I don't know if I am married or single, if I have children or not, if I have mother, father, brother, sister—well, all the rest. I have cuts and bruises all over me. I don't know if that passport is mine or forged. I don't know if my brain will be all right some day, if it is all right now, and I don't know if my arm will be straight, strong, usable. I am lonesome and occasionally I seem to be afraid. I don't know what I'm afraid of. I am afraid of Dr. Swendstrom, and I don't like that. He is ridiculously pretty and very solicitous— why should he frighten me? It seems idiotic. And this morning, while making conversation, which I damn well wish he'd leave unmade, he mentioned some man named Clarkson"—her eyes darkened—"and I almost jumped through the roof. It—it scared me. It *still* scares me."

"It? The man? The name?"

"How do I know? Since I don't know the man, it must be the name, I suppose. But to be frightened of nothing is to get more frightened. If you know what I mean."

"I know. But I find it hopeful. It represents a snatch of memory."

"Really? Well, while I'm at it let me add a few other things I'm angry at. I'm angry at doctors, or at my imprisonment between them. I don't like Swendstrom, but I have no choice in the matter, not on a ship. I think he's inept and foolish. For instance, can you see any reason why I shouldn't go on deck?"

Max could see no reason at all, but he contrived to look noncommittal.

"Well, Dr. Swendstrom seemed horrified by the suggestion. I went to all this trouble of getting dressed, and believe me when one's arm is in a sling dressing is both difficult and painful, and then he simply forbid me to go and get some air. No reasons, no answers. Just forbid. Who does he think he is?"

Max had no answer to that, either.

"And if you will forgive me, I have my doubts about you. I think you're nice enough, but what about my head, what about my mind? You don't seem to be getting anywhere with that." She took a deep breath and subsided.

Max took a breath, too. "Well," he said. "Where to start? At the beginning? At the beginning. If I can remember all the points. I asked to see your ticket and so I can answer the question as to where you're going. The ticket was purchased at the line's offices in Bond Street and it entitles you to first-class passage, cabin and bath, to Tokyo."

"And return?"

"No. But let's deal with what you have already asked, shall we? The cuts and bruises. The cuts seem to be very nearly healed. They weren't cuts so much as scratches—"

"Which is a damn funny result of falling down a flight of stairs."

"—they are already disappearing and they will leave no scars. The bruises will take a little longer, but bruises always do; they will heal. As for your 'head' as you put it, I examined you carefully; you had a minor concussion. The shock has subsided. Your arm sustained a simple break. The chances are overwhelmingly good that there will be no

84

aftereffects, except possibly that the arm will serve as a barometer. Ache before rain, that sort of thing.

"Now, as to me, at the risk of making excuses I shall—" He paused, smiled, and said, "I shall make two excuses. First of all, amnesia, with some very occasional exceptions, passes of itself. Long-term case histories are fairly rare in medical annals. Still, treatment is indicated. Roughly speaking there are three types of treatment, used individually or simultaneously—certain drugs, hypnosis, and free-association sessions—but, and we come to my second excuse, these are the special tools of the psychoanalyst. I do not practice psychoanalysis. I do not have the preferred drugs with me; free association lists, and certainly hypnosis, require considerably more experience than I can bring to them. To you. I consider it best to wait—for Genoa, if you wish, which is only two days away—and turn you over to a specialist."

"I see." Her eyes were wide. "That's all very interesting. Would I be permitted to get off at Genoa?"

"Permitted? You're a free agent. Certainly you'll be permitted. On the other hand, if you should prefer to stay and let nature take its probable course, the medical doctor on this ship, the accredited medical officer, might have the right to insist that you be removed. If he felt your condition was critical, he might have that right. Although, as I seem to tell people fairly often, I am not a marine lawyer."

"So I'm a free agent, but that twirp can boot me off the ship!"

"Now, look, that sort of feminine twist leaves me speechless. You were ready to be angry because you might be held aboard, and now you're in a temper because I suggest that you might be asked to disembark."

Elizabeth Smith smiled and looked very pleasant, although there was, Max thought, something wrong, awry, in her appearance. Was it the make-up, which seemed a bit too pale? Or the coiffure? The way the short dark hair curled around her face? Whatever, the impishness he had noted before was again in her smile. It was an attractive but unusual grin. She achieved little-girl wistfulness and womanly deviltry all with one tug of the lips. As if she were two people at once. He said, "Will you lunch with me?"

"An attractive offer. But you've forgotten that I am confined to quarters."

"What I meant was, will you invite me to lunch with you? Here?"

"Oh. Why, yes, thanks. It's a pleasant idea."

"Good. I'll ring for a menu. First, let's settle another of your questions. The passport. I don't have it any longer but I remember the signature."

"So do I. Namby-pamby."

"Well"—he reached into his jacket and brought out a pen and an envelope—"try it."

"Oh." She looked down at the pen and then up at him.

"It's your left arm that's unusable. And, remember?— you're right-handed."

"I wasn't going to refuse. Did you think I was going to refuse?" The clear eyes looked at him curiously. "Now, why would I do that? Why would you think I'd do that?"

"I don't know. Here—try it."

She took the pen, turned the envelope over and then, quickly, wrote "Elizabeth Smith." She pushed the envelope to its side so they could both inspect the result. Then she said, "It's the same. It's really the same. And it has that indefinable look of a signature, the look of habit. But"— she looked up at him, the eyes very intense, the musical voice very deep—"but it's sophomoric. It fits me about as well as this collection of little-girl suits and dresses, with their Peter Pan collars—not at all."

He realized then what the wrong note was: the green-wool dress was too young, too ingenue. It didn't suit her at all.

5

Max spent the afternoon answering his accumulated correspondence. Previously, the very idea of tackling the pile had caused him active nausea. But the sea, life on shipboard, had performed its usual trick of divorcement, plus its illusory sense of safety. This seemed another world; this *was* another world. It was a small planet, petty, lazy, gossipy, inert, but the stagnation merely reinforced its isolation from reality. The real world, the six continents, were not with them. The passengers would touch on land, and only then would they recognize the sense of unreality. They would look forward eagerly to each port, but on arrival they would almost immediately hanker for departure. They would go ashore with a comforting awareness of the fact that their world, their cocoon, their island of peace, waited impatiently at land's edge.

Here, in this never-never land of shipboard, the letters, as if from outer space, had lost their immediacy, and with it had gone their power to wound. They had not been intended to hurt: they were reminders of friendship, tactful and warm; some were outright statements of support and sympathy. There was even, among them, one from the ex-Mrs. Maxwell Owings. He supposed that it was an expression of sympathy, although it read more like an accusation. When he had first received and read it, its odd half-truths and total misses had irritated his nerves like an astringent on an open wound. Now, upon rereading, he found it amusing and even sympathetic:

. . . all nonsense. You are undoubtedly dour and misanthropic, *and* a misogynist, but underneath you are sensitive and even sympathetic, and you are neither cruel nor neglectful of duty. To accuse you of neglecting a patient, or a would-be patient, is idiotic—trouble with you is you take patients far too much to heart. I swear that in our few years together you had no less than a thousand neuroses and several hundred psychoses—these being the number of your patients. When I heard that you had dug yourself out of that dreary town and changed your specialty I was simply astonished, but I'll bet anything that it's made you a happier man. You may even be less morosely suicidal. I hope so. Anyway, as I was saying, this English thing is sheer nonsense, since your great trouble is a *lack* of ruthlessness. To accuse you of being ruthless is simply laughable. And to accuse you of worldliness, expediency, is worse; it's hysterically funny. Who could know better than I? Who could laugh louder? There is certainly no man alive who can disregard money more totally than you, damn it.

Looked at in a certain light, the letter was, to use her phrase, hysterically funny. First of all, he was a different man than the young Julie had known, so for *her* to psychoanalyze *him*, the present Max . . . And so far as "disregarding" money went, he had paid solid alimony once every month for five years—until three years earlier when she had remarried. Ah, well, she probably meant to be kind; they all did—the old friends, the professional contacts, the casual acquaintances. He wrote kind and grateful answers.

At four-thirty there was a tap on his door. To his response the white-jacketed steward opened the door and hovered there deferentially. "The captain's compliments, sir, and could the Herr Doktor spare him a minute at his earliest convenience?"

"Enter, enter." The captain, in glaring contrast to his behavior of the day before, rose courteously. "I am most sorry to take you from your tea." A further glaring contrast was provided by his shining dental plates. The room smelled strongly of brandy and black cigars.

"I don't take tea, so that's all right."

"Oh? I have called you only to advise you that I have —ah—mulled over your advice"—the word "advice" apparently came with difficulty, and Max shared the emotion; picturing the captain mulling over anyone's advice was a difficult feat—"and I have come to the conclusion that you are quite right. Therefore Scotland Yard is flying a man into Genua. We should arrive there, and he should consequently board, sometime on Saturday."

And that, Max thought, was one of the minor prices of temper.

The captain had made him angry, and so Max had goaded him into this step—this invasion of their safe, womblike world, this loss of peace and safety.

FRIDAY

SCHIFF *Tilburg.*
SHIP

Freitag den *18* ten *Januar*
Friday the   of *January*

38° 34'N Breite und *0'23' 0* Länge
       Latitude and   Longitude

Tages-Distanz: *391*   Seemeilen
Day's run: Nautical miles

Zurückgelegte Gesamtdistanz bis heute: *1445*
Total distance covered up to today:

Restdistanz bis: *Genua*
Distance still to be covered to: *525*

Having been threatened with bingo, Max had again skipped
the after-dinner activities. He had intended to finish his
letters but the inertia of shipboard had sent him to his

gently swaying bed before ten o'clock, and so he was in the dining room by seven-thirty, highly interested in the idea of breakfast.

There was no one at his table, and few people yet in the room. Among those few was Madame Hausman, also alone at her table. It was the first time since Max boarded that she had appeared before noon.

While he ate a healthy breakfast, he watched her. It was a safe occupation because her face, over the tea cup that seemed to represent her entire breakfast, was withdrawn, its tilted, hooded, eyes obviously examining a mysterious, far-away world. She wore a dark-red severely tailored suit, very handsome. Her long fingernails, much in evidence as her tapering fingers held the cup on high, were the exact color of the suit, and her right small finger was nearly covered by her only piece of jewelry, a glowing cabochon ruby. Her face, a delicate, mysterious mask, was the color of an Easter lily; it fine, unwrinkled texture suggested that it might also feel like a lily's petals. The black hair was drawn into a towering mass that looked Oriental but that Max vaguely recognized as being the latest Parisian exaggeration. Atop the coiffure was a shining ornament of green mother-of-pearl. The contrasting color was a final note of perfection, but Max decided that her beauty probably came largely from her character, her personality. She seemed so self-contained, so removed from trivia (one wondered that she had bothered to assemble the outfit), so remote from the nonsense of the Western world.

When Max poured his second cup of coffee she seemed to wake up. She called across the small space between his table and the captain's, "Good morning, Doctor. Why don't you have that coffee here with me?"

He rose happily and carried his cup to her table. He sat at her right, the round table with its widely spaced chairs permitting him a full view of her face. That close it was possible to concede that she might be more than thirty; it was not possible to believe that she was over forty.

92

She said, "It's cold, isn't it? I'm wearing this suit because it's cold." She had no trace of accent.

"It is cold. January, of course." He felt callow and shallow. He said, "This is the first time I've seen you at breakfast."

"First time I've been. I rarely get up before ten-thirty, sometimes eleven-thirty. But I'm up this morning to get into training, sort of. For next week."

The meaning escaped Max. "Next week?"

"If I get up early, it'll be easier next week. And I just must be up early then. Genoa, you know."

"You're anxious to go ashore? You have friends in Genoa?"

Her face made its first motion, a small but perfect smile. "The silk stores. They have simply beautiful silks in Italy, you know. It takes very little material to make a cheong-sam, you know. So I buy lengths here and have them made up home, in Hong Kong. Now, I know what you're think-ing—Hong Kong is famous for its beautiful materials, im-ported from all countries and tax free—but it's a small town, you know. If you buy your materials there, you keep meeting yourself. So to speak. So I buy the materials else-where and have my clothes made in Hong Kong. Not all of them, of course. This suit, now. This suit came from Saks Fifth. I was in New York last spring. Yours is a *wonderful* country, Doctor." Her face didn't change but an effect of vivacity became discernible. "Such *wonderful* stores. Bonwit's, Saks, Lord & Taylor, the small shops on Madison and in the crosstown streets. A *wonderful* coun-try!"

"New York, you mean. I am not a New Yorker."

"Well, I can't think why you sound defiant. *I* always think of it as being the whole country." The small smile warmed the ivory mask. "Very expensive, of course, but worth it. Now, in Paris I'm rarely tempted. Even more expensive, and infinite fittings. Although they do a good job of setting jewels. It's much cheaper at home, but I sometimes am very naughty and have my jewels reset in Paris. Good things are worth it, don't you think so?"

"Yes," Max said. "Certainly. So you're getting in training to do some shopping in Genoa? But we are not supposed to arrive there until afternoon, are we?"

"Yes, and then comes Sunday. But we'll have Saturday afternoon and most of Monday. So I'm getting ready, you know?"

"Indeed." Max could cheerfully have kicked Clarkson. Clarkson could have warned him; instead he had called a conversation with Madame Hausman an "indescribable experience that had to be lived through to be appreciated." In Max's opinion it was an experience in disillusionment that could have been thankfully lived without. He supposed that Clarkson wished to underline his sermon on the universality of people: So Much for the Mysterious East.

Max looked gratefully up at his bedroom steward, who had entered the dining room, glanced around, spotted Max, and was aiming toward him. The steward had an air of urgency, and Max experienced a doctor's slightly weary recognition of the probability that someone, somewhere, was suffering from something. Still, he thought, with unusual callousness, anything that served to deliver him from this conversation would be welcome. Anything.

Fritz reached his side and said, "Sorry, Herr Doktor, to disturb your breakfast—"

"Not a bit of it," Max said happily.

"—but could you please come along with me?"

"Certainly." Max rose, bowed with Oriental suavity over the beautiful ruby on the beautiful hand, murmured his regrets, and followed the steward out of the dining room.

In the foyer the steward said rapidly, "On deck, sir. I can't find the doctor. Dr. Swendstrom. He's not in his room. So early." He paused, seemed to make a try for coherence, and then gave it up. "A deckhand was looking for him. He found me. He stayed up there and I looked. But I can't find him. The doctor. Perhaps I should go to the purser first? Or the captain?"

94

"With what? Collect yourself, Fritz. If someone is hurt you are right to fetch a doctor first. One of the crew?"

"No. The Fräulein. On deck. Aft."

Max started up the stairs, and said over his shoulder, "Fräulein Gotthelf?"

"No, sir. The English one. Fräulein Elkin."

No, Max thought. Even as a deliverance from a conversation with Madame Hausman, harm to Miss Elkin was not worth it.

Fritz said, panting, "The pool."

Miss Elkin was not recognizable since she was hunched forward on her knees. One saw only a tumble of brown tweed in the center of the shining blue-green tiles. Beside her, sitting on his haunches, was a young man in dungarees. There was no blood.

Max started down the steps at the shallow end. He said to Fritz, still speaking over his shoulder, "Get my case. It's on the floor beside the dressing table. On the left as you face it." To the anxious-looking deckhand who still crouched beside the bundle of brown tweed, "Did you touch her?"

The boy—he was little more than that—struggled to understand the English, apparently succeeded, and then struggled to reply. "No touch. Lift the head."

Max knelt on the other side of Miss Elkin and also lifted her head. Then he saw the blood, but it came not from a visible wound but from her nose. Miss Elkin had a nose-bleed, and through it she was breathing stertorously. He turned her gently, getting her out of the prayerlike position, equalizing the flow of blood, and then ran his hand over the back of her head. Yes; she had the beginnings of what would be an enormous egg at the base of the skull.

He said to the boy, "It's not long since you found her?"

"*Nein. Zehn Minuten.* Since ten minutes. She scream. Then I hear the sound when she—she—"

"Fell? Hit the tiles?"

"*Ja.* I come fast. I go, see Fritz. He go. I come back. Ten minutes."

Fritz came back again, at a run, case in hand. Max said, "Thanks. Go to the doctor's office, see if there's a stretcher. You understand 'stretcher'?"

"Yes, sir."

"And send this boy to look for Dr. Swendstrom." He turned his attention to Miss Elkin.

Miss Elkin was deposited on her bed. She did not regain consciousness, but she would be all right. A concussion, Max thought—another concussion. But, fortunately, an even milder concussion. And more bruises. Her knees were badly bruised, and her wrists would be swollen.

The deckhand did not find the doctor. Max thanked him, and sent Fritz to report to the captain. Then he himself set out to find the purser.

But the purser seemed unfindable.

2

The superintendent said, "Ah, there you are, Medford. Sorry to be so urgent, but the post-mortem report on the Thames body has just come in and it is, ah, interesting." In line with his new departure from normal the superintendent looked positively smug. "The autopsy report was delayed, as you know, and now the reason for their slowness has become clear. Death *was* due to strangulation, but they had decided to be very careful to be sure of that—because a bullet was found in the body. The bullet has now been identified by the lab as having come from Barkland's gun. Thames man was apparently shot with it, almost harmlessly, and then finished by hand."

A very rich cream on his whiskers, Medford thought. He said, "Link established, eh, sir?"

"Certainly is." He relinquished smug dignity and beamed. "Now perhaps you can tie it all up."

"Quite." Medford felt less happy than ever.

"Don't you think?" The superintendent's voice was sharp.

"Well, perhaps."

"But you're the one who's always splicing these bits into one strand, or trying to."

"Forgive me, but—'always'? I don't think I do it 'always.' "

"Well, all right"—the super sounded like a child who, suspecting the worst, nevertheless wishes to be told that Santa Claus exists—"but why, dammit, do you object to trying this time?"

A very good question, Medford thought. Why was he pulling away from the suggestion of one neat crime? He thought it out, slowly and aloud: "I think my reluctance to see it all as being easily tieable is because of the multiplicity of the strands." He caught a glimpse of the super's face and looked away before he could be scorched. "Forgive me for pursuing your analogy, but it fits. We have a murdered Dr. Barkland; a stethoscope-equipped body in the Thames; the Terrence Clinic affair in the background; a dead doctor—poisoned, not shot—killed in Dutch waters; and even the probably extraneous Dr. Owings, with his dubious background. Now a link has been established between the first two bodies. Well, fine. But when it comes to putting it all together, if we ever do, I suspect that although the strands may touch, they will not actually splice. I suspect that there have been many occurrences, many motives, perhaps even many crimes, but not just one grand plan. The edges may touch, probably intermesh, but not a neat splice." He shook his head.

Asperity was written large on the super's face. He said, "Here I have been, somewhat embarrassed at making the assumption that these deaths were related, feeling that the assumption was more like you than me. Now, in a completely negative way, you have put us back on familiar footing: given a *fact* proving a relationship, you make one of your usual vaulting assumptions, this time a negative one. Can you give me one reason for the leap? Just *one?*"

"Yes, I think so. The gun. The gun was Dr. Barkland's, so the murderer didn't come prepared. Unpremeditated murder, it would seem. It is therefore possible that the Thames corpse witnessed Barkland's death, and was shot in self-protection. Against being identified. Then the murderer ran out of bullets and strangled him. But an unpremeditated murder attempted by gun and finished manually is farther than ever from a poisoning at sea."

The superintendent examined him coldly for at least five seconds. "Assumption," he then said. "You will please investigate the murder of all these doctors, as previously instructed."

SATURDAY

SCHIFF _Tilburg_
SHIP

Sonnabend den _19_ ten _Januar_
Saturday the of _January_
_42° 20' N_ Breite und _06° 11'_ _0_ Länge
Latitude and Longitude

Tages-Distanz: _348_ Seemeilen
Day's run: Nautical miles

Zurückgelegte Gesamtdistanz bis heute: _1793_
Total distance covered up to today:

Restdistanz bis: _Genua_ _177_
Distance still to be covered to:

Max turned from the daily record of the ship's run in time
to catch the purser, who was scurrying down the alleyway
in an obvious attempt to avoid just such an eventuality.

"Hello," Max called out with cheerful cruelty, and watched happily while the purser slowed, decided he was caught, and returned slowly.

"*Gut* morning," he said miserably. "How is your patient?"

"Which one?" Max asked with a feeling that the reminder that two of the purser's passengers were patients would not soothe him. He added, "Isn't three hundred forty-eight miles rather a bad run?" Strike from all sides, was his current batting stance.

"Bad weather," the purser said lugubriously.

"Really? I thought the weather was pleasant."

"You are not a man of the sea." He achieved a kind of dignity that took Max by surprise. Faced with the recumbent Miss Elkin on the previous morning—after a multideck search had produced him—he had shown no dignity whatever. He had seemed to want to deny her injury, to pretend to her nonexistence. He had not wanted to acknowledge that she or Max existed, and the hint that an investigation into who had bopped her must follow had produced a frenzy of denial out of him. She had clearly *fallen*, he announced. "Clearly?" Max had asked. "You saw her fall?"

"Of course not!"

"Then you saw her after she had fallen?"

"This—this theory of yours—is the first I have learned of the—the accident!"

"A fall is not a theory—"

"My Englisch is bad."

"Your English is excellent.—And just as a fact cannot be described as a theory neither can an attack be described as an accident.—The captain seems to be unavailable. Where is he?"

"I don't understand."

"*Wo ist der Kapitän?*"

"*Nicht sehr gut.* He is not—not very well."

"Seasick?"

"You joke."

"I demand to see the captain."

But the captain had remained unavailable, the purser had remained undignified, and Miss Elkin had remained unconscious. Dr. Swendstrom had also remained unfindable until Max pointed out that the ship had not the dimensions of the *Queen Elizabeth*. . . . Max had been somewhat confused by his own insistence on having Swendstrom produced. What help could he expect of that type? But he was in a temper, and when Swendstrom had finally appeared and tch-tch-ed handsomely, Max had been even angrier. However, surrounded as they were by stewards and stewardesses, there was little he could say. And, for that matter, what could he have said if he and Swendstrom had been alone?

His anger was pointless: Miss Elkin was, as he would have put it in a hospital report, "resting comfortably," and there was nothing to do but wait.

While he was waiting, occasionally holding Miss Elkin's hand, Max realized he had fallen madly in love with Miss Elkin. It was not sexual love, it would not end in passionate romance, it would not even be described by the world as "love"—but he loved her devotedly and some of his frenzy of anger, at the purser, the captain, Swendstrom, the whole damn ship, sprang from his devotion. Poor babe, he said to himself, looking down at Miss Elkin's blood-smeared white face. No woman, he admitted, had ever been less of a "babe"; even her glow had gone out. But she was a dear and no one should have hit her on the noodle.

Clarkson supplied the comfort. Max had barked "Come in" to an uncharacteristically timid knock, had looked up expecting to find a stewardess, and had been greeted by a woebegone-looking Clarkson.

"What are you doing here?" Max demanded ungraciously.

"Rumor hath it—"

"Spare me the Biblical phraseology."

"That's not Biblical." Clarkson looked wounded. "That's a preamble to an admission of gossip-mongering."

"Well, Miss Elkin is not a fit subject for gossip."

Clarkson had looked confused, amused, and unhappy. "Of course not," he said softly. "How is she?"

"Probably all right. 'Resting comfortably' is what we always say at this point."

"And you are not resting comfortably at all."

"They refuse to do anything," Max said furiously.

"There's something they can do?"

"Admit she was conked, find out who did it, and turn him over to me."

"I see." Clarkson looked down at Miss Elkin. "Is she drugged?"

"Hasn't regained consciousness."

"Is that alarming?"

"No. Pulse almost normal, heart . . . Well, she's okay."

"Oh." Clarkson sat down on the opposite side of the bed, cautiously, as if fearing he would be denied permission. "She looks like hell."

"She was conked," Max said furiously.

They had spent the afternoon there, one on each side. Eventually Miss Elkin opened her dimly blue eyes, which looked even more dim than usual. She examined their faces, smiled slightly, and they watched as the glow came back. "Hurts," she said, saw their look of concern, and quickly added, "Not much."

"I'll fix it," Max said. "What happened?"

Miss Elkin's expressive face performed one of its magnificent displays of multiple emotions: confusion, awareness, memory, decision. "What happened?" she repeated. "That should be my question, shouldn't it?" Then she smiled again and went back to sleep. This time she retained the glow, even as she snored gently.

"She *was* conked?" Clarkson asked.

"Indubitably," Max said, in glorious, irritated English.

"I ask you," the purser said with Germanic phlegmatism, "how is your patient? Your *new* patient."

"She is as well as can be expected. . . . In view of the

miserable display of mileage during the last twenty-four hours, when can we expect to arrive in Genoa?"

"As early as can be expected. About five o'clock."

2

"She was conked," Max said furiously. Thirty hours had done nothing to mitigate his anger.

What the devil? Medford said to himself. It was his twentieth internal repetition of the phrase within a half hour. This Owings was a man he thought might usually be intelligent, cool, and dependable, but he was currently none of those things so far as Medford could discover. And Owings' anger seemed disproportionate. If, Medford conceded, one had the right to judge "proportions" when dealing with a stranger.

Medford gazed through the lounge's window at a wet and dismal view of the high wall that seals off Genoa's wharfs. Then he said, his voice gentle, "Conked?"

"Hit over the head. Blunt instrument. Bopped. Have you never met an American, never come into contact with crude American slang?"

"Ah," said Medford, with an almost burlesque of awareness, "it's American slang! So she was hit over the head. According to you."

"Back of head. You may not have heard of American slang, Inspector, but you must have heard of blunt instruments."

"Quite," Medford said. Could this rather severely handsome and youngish man be in love with the schoolma'armish old maid Medford had spoken to briefly? It seemed unlikely. And was this the man bruited about England as being heartless? He wondered (chiding himself still again for leaping even to the low point of surmise) if, quite to the contrary, this were not one of that breed of dedicated doctors one sometimes met. They always seemed a bit off balance to Medford. He said slowly, with a little carefully applied cruelty, "I did not come aboard to examine the tribulations of Miss—ah—Elkin. My questions have not concerned Miss Elkin. But I seem to hear little except about Miss Elkin. So, since we persist in discussing the lady, or rather her fall, may I ask why you are so positive that she was—ah—bopped? Conked? The purser dismisses the matter as a fall. And the purser says the ship's doctor agrees with him."

"How interesting! Especially since the purser didn't arrive for half an hour after she was bashed, and by the time the doctor arrived she had almost recovered."

"But *you* were on the scene?"

"I got there about ten minutes after she hit the pool's bottom, according to the seaman who heard her scream and actually heard her land."

"Well, then, Doctor, let us return to my question of five minutes ago: Why are you so positive she was hit? It seems to me you weren't any more of an eye witness than the purser or the doctor."

"At least I saw where she fell."

"And that is pertinent?"

"Intensely, since she was on her knees bang in the middle of the pool's floor. In the *middle*. Did you ever see anyone fall downward, outward, and over about six feet?"

"No," Medford said quietly. "I didn't. Not into a space that deep. It seems quite impossible to me. She could of course have jumped—"

"That is flatly idiotic."

"—in order to arrive in that position, but from what everyone says and from my own necessarily hasty judgment of the lady, that seems to be an unlikely assumption. Ah—idiotic."

"Well, then." Owings had the grace to look mildly uncomfortable. "Something else, then: Her knees are badly bruised and both wrists are strained. Landed on her hands and knees. But has an egg on the back of her head. Can't have it both ways."

But the fight seemed to be over and it occurred to Max that his success had hardly been worth the spleen he had put into it. This policeman looked intelligent, was polite if a bit frigid, and might usually be very pleasant, but at the moment Max found him (and almost everyone else, he realized) thoroughly irritating. I am caught, he thought, between so many fires that it is a miracle I haven't become even more explosive. I didn't want a policeman, but I demanded one. Now that I've got him, I'm egging him on. Miss Elkin isn't seriously hurt, and . . . the truth finally came over him: it was probably his suspicion as to who had hit her that was infuriating him. "What," he asked in a more equable tone, "does *she* say? Miss Elkin? When I last saw her she was asleep, but I gather you've talked to her?"

"Yes. She says she has no idea what happened. She doesn't remember."

There was a little silence and then Medford said softly, "You find that odd, doctor?"

Max paused before replying, and when he did speak he gave the impression of choosing his words carefully: "No. Medically speaking, no. As I explained once before this week—regarding my other patient, the one whose case you actually came aboard to handle—a little blank period is usual when one is hit on the head. It's called retrograde amnesia. Perfectly natural."

The new pause was Medford's, and it was now he who spoke cautiously: "The other patient? The one I came aboard . . . How did you know, Dr. Owings, why I came aboard?"

"The captain told me you were coming."

"I see. Or rather, I don't quite. The captain didn't mention my expected arrival to either his chief mate or to the purser, or to anyone else in authority that I can uncover, so—forgive me—why did he confide in you?"

"Because I had demanded the investigation."

"I see," Medford said untruthfully. "Into the condition of your patient? You thought—what? That he had been attacked? Like Miss Elkin?"

"Ah." Max stared at him. "You have seen the captain?"

What the devil? Medford thought for the twenty-first time. Something had slipped but he had no idea what or why. He chose pure truth: "I have not met the captain. He did not see fit to await my arrival. I understand that he has gone, um, shopping with a lady. And he left no word for me, and no hint to anyone aboard that I was coming. Except to you." He paused. Then he said, "I have not yet had time to examine the passports of those aboard. Obviously, since I've been here a bare half-hour. But the purser is putting a room at my disposal and delivering the passports there. Reluctantly. In fact, to tell you the truth, I think he is stalling about until the captain returns and gives permission. Which is understandable, I suppose, and I am making no issue of it. Still, in the absence of passports, may I ask when you boarded?"

"Sure. In Southampton."

"That was the fourteenth?"

"Exactly. Five long days ago."

And the ship's doctor, the *original* ship's doctor—damn it, there *were* too many doctors in this bisque—the original ship's doctor died the night of the twelfth, seven long days ago. So who was "the other patient"? Into a mind full of doctors, blurred with doctors, seasoned with doctors, Medford dipped, stirred, and ladled up a question: "Your patient, the other one, is he a doctor?"

"Inspector Medford, 'he' is a 'she.' She has no idea who or what she is, and neither have I."

"Oh." He would go back to school, Medford told himself. To fall into the oldest trap in the world would have been bad, but this one wasn't even baited. The man hadn't tried to trick him; Medford had simply opened his silly mouth without thinking. "Quite," Medford said. " 'No idea who she is'? Amnesia?"

"Yes."

"From an injury?"

"Yes."

"Self-inflicted? Accidental? Ah, no, you said you had demanded an investigation, so you presume an attack? Since she has amnesia, it *is* presumption?"

"Not quite."

"Come, come, Doctor. You weren't so monosyllabic before."

"I trusted you before."

"And you don't now? You, like the purser, are going to wait for the captain to vouch for me?"

"Of all the people in this world I don't trust, the captain is Abou ben Adhem."

"Ah? Well, then, would you like to see my credentials?"

Max looked at the man who lounged beside him with an air of ease that wasn't in the least misleading. He was a couple of inches taller than Max, perhaps six feet tall, but otherwise physically much like him—slender, wiry, alert, healthy in body, and similarly alert, wiry, and wary in mind. His black cap of hair was much darker than his skin, and his skin was much darker than his light gray eyes. His teeth were very, very white. And despite all that contrast he managed to be rather unobstrusive. And—trustworthy.

"No," Max said. "I don't need to see your credentials. But I would like you to answer a question. Why did the captain send for you if not to investigate the case behind Miss Smith?"

"Miss Smith? The amnesia victim? Well, now, the captain *didn't* send for me. As I understand it from my superiors he was advised by *his* superiors that I would arrive.

"The dirty liar," Max said softly. Then he laughed, also softly. "So you have not been conjured up by me. You are simply a trick of fate. Very amusing. Well, what is the fateful event that brought you?"

Medford's silver eyes were neutral. Then he smiled, and Max was surprised by the warmth the slight smile gave his face. He had been told that his own smile performed the same transformation, and he saw for the first time what was meant by "transformation." He thought it likely that his own "transformation" gave less impression of serene balance. Medford said, and the smile did not carry to his voice, "No. Sorry, but for the time being I will not answer that question."

"Then we're at a dead end, aren't we?" The man's warmth cut off easily. Max felt actually, physically cold.

"Why a dead end? Tell me about your Miss Smith. You asked the captain for someone to investigate, and no matter how roundabout, here I am. Perhaps it is fortuitous."

Perhaps it was. Perhaps he had flouted fate too often. Max said abruptly, "Come see her. Miss Smith. Then we can talk about her and her experiences."

Medford rose with casual ease. "Off we go. I suspect she has personality, no? And the story will make better sense after I've met her?"

"Well, true personality is what she has lost, of course. Partly you're right, but also I am overdue on my visit. I go down at least twice a day, mornings and afternoons. This morning she was prepared to tear the legs off giants, and I don't want to add to her upset."

"A temper?" Medford followed Max down the curving stairs.

"At times. Her complaint this morning seemed more feminine than bad-tempered. As far as I could gather, if they didn't let her off at Genoa she was going to jump overboard and come back with the whole *carabinieri*. But if they insisted she disembark, she was going to chain herself to something—the anchor chain, I think—and demand her rights. We've been tied up for almost an hour and I've not yet seen her either pulling or pushing." He knocked on the door of Cabin 42, and then abruptly turned to face Medford. "And I suspect that I know why she has been so quiet. You'll—"

A high voice said, "Who is it?"

"Dr. Owings and a guest. May we come in?"

"Yes." The one word contrived hesitancy.

She was sitting in the corner that got the least light. She had on still another of the little-girl, Peter-Pan-collared dresses, this one in pale tan. Her eyes seemed abnormally large, her pale face pathetically small, and the dark curls that circled her face seemed almost too heavy for such smallness to support. The arm in its sling lay limply against her ribs.

Max said gently, "Good evening, Miss Elizabeth. This gentleman is from the English police. His name is Inspector Medford."

She caught her breath.

Medford offered a little bow.

"From the police?" The voice went so high that it nearly cracked. "But why?"

"If you were pushed you'll want to talk to him. You're sure you *were* pushed, and you wanted—"

"Pushed? No, no. I don't think so, do you? I mean, not really."

"No," Max said instantly. "Not really. Why don't you rest now? I'll drop down later. Perhaps you'll want to take a walk around Genoa."

"Oh, no," she said. "No, not now."

"No," Max agreed. "Not now. But you might want to later."

3

"You'd make a jolly good reporter," Medford said. "Have the feeling I was there."

Owings smiled. "A trick. I've always had it. The accuracy won't last long. I can't repeat like that after a month or two. But it did help me to get through the University and medical school in a minor blaze of glory. My scholastic standing was greater than my brains because of my ability to parrot lectures."

Medford wondered how much of that was modesty. He said, "And I take it that *was* a report? A parroting? No opinions, merely a statement of what you saw and of what people said?"

"Exactly."

"Excuse me, Herr Doktor. Would you and the gentleman like a drink?" Heinz, the lounge steward, was standing in front of them. Max noted that the lights had been turned on. He said, "Yes, please. Scotch and water. Inspector?"

"The same. And has the captain returned?"

"No, sir."

"Has the purser assigned a room to me?"

"I'll find out, sir."

Max looked at the two or three passengers who had filtered in for pre-dinner cocktails and said, "Would you like to go down to my cabin, Inspector?"

"Very much."

"You'll bring the drinks, Heinz?"

"Yes, Herr Doktor."

They went back down the stairs and into the quiet of Max's cabin. When they were comfortably installed and supplied with their drinks, Medford said, "Well, then, according to this report of yours, to its tone, at any rate, she probably fell down the stairs. Her mental condition is unstable, and was probably so before the fall. And yet you wanted the matter investigated. So you have some other ideas, beyond sheer reportage. Yes?"

"No. Not really."

"No? But then why did you 'demand an investigation'? I quote you."

"I heard the quotation marks. But if those were my words, I was being less than usually accurate. I think the captain simply irritated me into saying far more than I had intended. You haven't met the captain; you'll understand when you meet him."

"Which reminds me that I haven't met the doctor, either. This is an annoyingly deserted ship, from my point of view.—Well, now, if I may continue to quote: you were irritated into saying 'far more than you had intended.' What had you intended to say?"

"I intended to offer him the courtesy of a report."

"A report on what?"

"The condition of Miss Smith."

"The suspicious condition of Miss Smith?"

"Well . . ."

"Because, Doctor, you used the words 'criminal attack.'"

"I was annoyed." Max looked not only annoyed but stubborn.

"Now, look," Medford said, "you may not have been aware of it, but you have made out a case against a particular person."

"*I* have?"

"Yes, Doctor. As you relate the facts, I am led to the inescapable conclusion that you think—perhaps subconsciously?—that the ship's doctor pushed Miss Smith down the stairs."

"The *doctor!*" Owings passed annoyance and achieved outrage. "I have said no such thing! It would be, at the least, unethical, and beyond that—"

"Unethical? Come, come, Doctor. Ethics, in your profession, apply"—Medford paused, thinking of his comment to the superintendent, "they stick together like a guildhall of Musketeers"—"or *should* apply to medicine, and to doctors as medical men. Ethics do not apply to crime, or to doctors as criminals."

"But I did *not* say the doctor was a criminal!"

Medford examined his outraged face and decided there was even more than outrage there. What was it, the emotion behind that shocked face? He didn't know. But he thought again that Owings seemed to be overdedicated; perhaps his reaction was a facet of that quality. "Now, listen," he said quietly, "to what you have told me: Elizabeth Smith has developed two personalities, correct?"

"Yes."

"In the grip of one she is afraid of the doctor, in the other she dislikes him."

"Enormously inconclusive. Of anything. And she is not normal, probably not before the fall, certainly not now. Not in the meek personality, not in—"

"Wait, please, Doctor. That is just a beginning. Let me list all your points, however unconsciously you made them. Second, he gave her too much of a drug, and was reluctant to stop, although you seem to have considered it medically unnecessary. Third, he kept her boxed up in her room. You haven't said much about that, but it is transparently clear that you find it equally unnecessary. Her mirrors were probably stolen. As a policeman I have a bitter understanding of coincidence, but it does have limits. So I suggest to you that the doctor doesn't want Miss Smith recognized, by herself or anyone else."

"Amnesia can't be induced. Certainly not without hypnotism and a number of other things he hasn't done."

"Perhaps he meant to kill her. Or to harm her seriously enough so that he could bandage her up and keep her incommunicado."

Max shook his head. "I think you are falling into the error of *your* profession, looking for crime where it simply doesn't exist. You haven't proved she didn't slip. You can't indict a man for something that may never have happened."

"True. But to support your reason for reporting to the captain you made the point that the doctor said her cuts, which were really scratches, were probably caused by the edges of the risers as she fell. And you added that the stairs are carpeted and that there are rubber edges on each tread."

"Inconclusive." Owings added, in a newly quiet, unemotionally certain tone: "I did not see the *original* cuts. They *could* have been caused by a fall. Under oath, on a witness stand, I would be absolutely incapable of suggesting that they were not caused by a fall."

"Quite," Medford said. "The *original* cuts. Whether you intend it or not, whether you realize it or not, you constantly differentiate between the *original* mischance Miss Smith suffered, and suggest that it *may* have been an accident, may *not* have been an attack, and the *second* incident, about which you harbor no doubt whatever: you consider it to have been an attack. Her wounds had reopened, but they were not serious enough to do anything of the sort. So they hadn't 'reopened'; they were newly inflicted. They were new, they were slight, they had probably been inflicted by a razor blade and could not have been caused by a fall—I am talking about the scratches you *saw*, not the ones that were bandaged when you first viewed Miss Smith—the ones you saw could not have been caused by a fall, unless it were on broken glass. That is the gist of what you have said."

"Well," Max said slowly, "it *is* more or less what I have said. I didn't intend any such conclusions to be drawn, but it's more or less what I said. However, it still doesn't prove anything against the doctor. You force me, in his defence, to be totally unethical—because, Inspector, he might be a medical idiot who simply made a mistake."

"I wonder," Medford said, "about your crisp statement of facts. Your factual report of what happened. Were you hypnotized when you made it? Because *I* seem to have heard what you said, but *you* don't seem to have heard yourself. You reported, Dr. Owings, that the ship's doctor *said* there were scratches—'cuts and abrasions'—and then he *said* the 'wounds had reopened,' those wounds you hadn't seen. But even if he is a medical idiot, that couldn't have been true, because you looked at the girl's right hand the first time you saw her—before this business of 'reopening' arose, and *there wasn't a mark on it*. But when the 'wounds' had 'reopened' her right hand was cut."

"True," Owings muttered. "True. Something was bothering me. I suppose that was it."

"Your door was locked. It took a long time before you could get it opened. That permitted the necessary time for the scratching to be done. Then, when you both entered, the ship's doctor reacted before you, although he was physically behind you. Do you think his reflexes are all that good?"

Max smiled wryly. "That's a little fine."

"True. It's just one of the many bits that appear in your story. There's another one, less fine. You went to get your bag, your medical case, because you were going to examine the girl. But he had already done his examining and treating, hadn't he?"

"Yes, why?"

"He came along with a case, however?"

"Well, yes, he did."

"A *Red Cross kit?* All prepared to bandage?"

Owings opened his mouth, and then left it that way. After several seconds he managed to get it closed. Then, slowly, stubbornly, he started to shake his head. "Look," he said, "look. You've built all this up on the statement of a single witness—me. And I'm not prepared to stand behind it. Because there's something else, very much in Swendstrom's favor. Elizabeth Smith suggested I didn't like the young man, and although I certainly wouldn't admit it to a patient, she was right. But my reasons are nonsensical. Swendstrom's teeth are capped, which really caps his beauty and irritates the hell out of me, and he uses a strong scent, and as a doctor . . ." He shook his head. "Still, my dislike undoubtedly colors my—"

"Swendstrom?" Medford sat forward. "The doctor's name is Swendstrom? What's his first name?"

"I—don't know. Well, I think I did hear it. Neil? No, Nils. Why? Hadn't I mentioned his name?"

"No. No, you hadn't." Medford added slowly, "I'll tell you one thing, in case you have a doubt: he is a qualified doctor."

The knock on the door was followed by a panting

Heinz. He said, "*Bitte.* Come. The Doctor Swendstrom."

Medford stood up.

Heinz ignored him. His attention was fastened on Max. "Dead," he said. "Or dying. You come?"

Owings shot out of the room as if by rocket, and Heinz seemed to fly along on his coat tails.

Medford did not sit down.

He stood, looking into nowhere, thinking hard but with bemusement. He had just had a very odd interview. The discussion had been, in fact, unique in his experience.

Dr. Owings had supplied him with a complete and damning list of facts, and then had tried to disown them, had, at least, fought against any acceptance of them. Why? The possibilities were endless, but the simplest, the one that sprang to mind, was that Owings wished to implicate the ship's doctor but didn't wish to admit it. Medford shook his head; he didn't believe that was true, but if the superintendent had asked him why not, he wouldn't be able to answer. (That was his rule of thumb for judging whether he was sinking too deep into the realm of intuition.) So it remained a possibility. A second possibility was the business of "ethics"; perhaps the doctor simply found it impossible to implicate or undermine a confrere. Medford shook his head again; he didn't believe that either. (The hell with the superintendent.) Perhaps Owings was trying to involve the ship's doctor because he himself had scratched up the girl? No. That notion could probably be destroyed, Medford decided, by the march of events, and even to the satisfaction of a handful of superintendents. Perhaps someone else had done it, and Owings was trying to supply a goat?

Medford started for the door, moving slowly. Whatever had impelled the doctor to offer a report that he did not wish accepted (or seemed not to wish accepted—?) he had now withdrawn a great, great distance from that report. Because Dr. Owings had said that Medford had built the case against the ship's doctor "on the statement of a single witness." Himself; Owings. And, Owings had added, "I am not prepared to stand behind it."

Was that actually a threat to disown his statements?

4

An additional ten minutes elapsed before Medford got to Swendstrom's cabin because he was held up by a young, very beautiful, and intensely unhappy police officer who made painstakingly sure that Medford was indeed Medford. Passport, Scotland Yard credentials, driver's license, and several further cards of identity seemed only partially to reassure him, but he finally handed over an elaborately sealed cablegram. (Medford hadn't seen red sealing wax, complete with crested intaglio, in many a year.) The cable had been sent to Genoa police headquarters with an accompanying cable advising them that they were to deliver it personally to Detective-Inspector Medford aboard the *Tilburg*.

The Italian police had been alerted, before Medford's arrival, to the fact that he was due, and they had offered their co-operation. Medford had proceeded to headquarters before boarding the *Tilburg*, and there he had politely but with necessary firmness refused everything from a glass of wine through a flying squad of magnificently uniformed assistants. But now their co-operation *was* being requested —as messenger boys. This particular bobby was therefore suffering from wounded dignity.

Medford displayed elaborate gratitude and asked the young man to wait in tones that suggested his comprehension of the fact that Genoa might fall apart as a result of his absence. The officer seemed mollified but insisted (while Medford ached to read the cable) on offering his own help, his superiors', and the mayor's. That fervency disposed of, Medford made his apologies and opened the envelope:

THAMES FINGERPRINT DEVELOPED CLEARLY STOP WORK-
ING ON IDENTIFICATION STOP ANY CONNECTION YOUR
END QUESTION MARK

The signature was entirely clear, and it brought forth Medford's slight but relieving smile. The superintendent had unprecedentedly done his own cabling and, equally without precedent, had dispatched a totally unnecessary cable. There was no need to mention the fingerprint until and if—a large "if"—it was identified. The purpose of the cable lay in its question mark.

Medford felt that he was entitled to a little time. He had been aboard the *Tilburg* less than three hours, had not yet been given official co-operation, and was being presented with innumerable prone bodies who either were or were not the subjects of a policeman's business, either were or were not connected with his mission, either were or were not a matter of his jurisdiction even if they were criminal cases.

But even in those couple of hours—Medford experienced a small tinkle of excitement—he had established the "connection at his end." He accepted the form the policeman had brought and block-printed a reply:

PROBABLE CONNECTION HERE ALSO STOP NEW MEDICAL
OFFICER NAMED NILS SWENDSTROM SAME NAME AS ONE
OF THREE FREED IN TERRENCE CLINIC TRIALS STOP
SWENDSTROM NOW ILL WILL ADVISE FURTHER SHORTLY
MEDFORD

The ship's doctor's cabin was very small, very clean, and totally impersonal. Even in only five days, Medford thought, one usually put some mark of personality on a room. Then he realized that the doctor had indeed done

that, if not to the eyes at least to the nostrils of a visitor;
there was a strong floral scent in the room.

Owings said absently, "Oh, there you are," and then ignored him.

Medford peered over Owings' shoulder through the loop
of a stethoscope at what looked like a corpse, a black-
wavy-haired, dead-white-faced, beautiful corpse. It was
fully dressed except for uniform jacket. Medford said, "Is
he dead?"

"Damn near." Owings abandoned a white limp wrist,
yanked open an eyelid, and then, shockingly, began slap-
ping the white face. The head lolled limply.

Medford got out of the way, which, in that room, meant
that he backed two feet against the only piece of furniture
outside of the bed and a chair—a desk-bureau-dressing-
table affair. He turned and looked at it, and then, after a
moment of self-communion, opened the center drawer.
Shirts. The drawers beneath contained the rest of the ward-
robe—socks, undershirts, underpants, handkerchiefs. There
was not a snapshot, a letter, a postcard, a snatch of paper.

Medford looked to his left. Beside the sink hung a jacket;
it had two wide gold stripes around each sleeve, caduceus
above them. He contemplated it only briefly.

There were about ten shillings in change in the outer
pocket; no keys. The left-hand inner pocket produced a
wallet, and a single envelope. He peeked: there was a letter
inside. The wallet contained a hundred and two pounds.
No driver's license. No identity card. It did boast a snapshot—a very blond woman smiling in the sun. Her arms
were around two towheaded boys of perhaps seven and
nine. Neither the woman nor the children were particularly attractive although all three radiated blond good
health.

Medford fingered the letter and looked thoughtfully
at the longish figure on the bed. Owings had now got the
man under the covers, and the face resting against the sheet
was the same tone of bluish-white. The black hair seemed
shockingly dark. Mendel's Law? Medford thought, and

then, in the absence of the superintendent to do it for him, chided himself. The snapshot could be of a sister, a cousin, a friend, any damn one.

A knock on the door brought him back from his contemplation of the superintendent's scorn over such leaps. Owings said, "Come in," and to Medford, "Better get out. This"—he nodded at the elderly woman in white who was standing in the open doorway; she was carrying an apparently heavy tray which was covered with a white napkin—"is the stewardess recommended as a practical nurse. There isn't room for the three of us, and anyway I'm going to pump him out. Very nasty business."

"He was poisoned?" Medford asked.

"Something in his insides, yes. Food poisoning, perhaps."

"You'll keep a sample?"

"A specimen? Of course."

"Will a hint help?"

"A hint about what's in him?" Owings let go of the doctor's wrist and turned around in surprise. "It certainly might. How could you—"

"I couldn't. Not really. But if it doesn't cause a dangerous pause or something of the sort, try a remedy for a common household antiseptic and preservative." He named it.

Medford leaned his long body against the outside wall of the doctor's cabin and regarded the envelope. It had a neat postmark, out of Hamburg, 12th January, 18:30 P.M., and was addressed to "Dr. Nils Swendstrom, 12 B, Short Ridge Road, London, S.W. 6, England." It had been sent by express mail.

The letterhead inside was familiar, and the signature equally familiar: that of the *Tilburg's* head office and the shipping line's secretary. It said:

My dear Doctor Swendstrom,
    Thank you for your prompt reply cable accepting the emergency post. Only such a state of emergency could

cause me in the name of my company to make so pre-emptory a request.

On this day I have been notified that the medical officer has died aboard a ship of our line, the M. S. *Tilburg*.

The ship was expected to sail tomorrow, but will now lie over in Southampton until Monday at noon; the day after tomorrow, the fourteen. Will you, as I asked in my cable, undertake a single trip as Chief Medical Officer of the *Tilburg?* (We can then discuss the future upon your return.) We have no one available to fly out at once, and you have been highly recommended.

The letter continued with a rundown of the *Tilburg's* itinerary, the medical officer's normal duties, the salary he would receive, the fact that he would be permitted to charge private patients "at reasonable fees, to be retained by yourself." It concluded:

If you will contact our London agents, P. L. Conway & Son, Ltd., Old Bond Street, on Monday morning at seven-thirty o'clock, they will be present to supply the first installment of the fee, a ticket to Southampton, your temporary authorization, all papers and details. I am assured that you will receive this letter early on Sunday."

And it was signed, as had been the colorless biography of the deceased Dr. Otto Ulmann, "Kurt Von Winckel, Secretary."

Medford used the ship-to-shore phone and requested a personage from the police station; he hoped it would not be the same one.

Then, at the table in his cabin, he drafted two cables.

To the superintendent:

SWENDSTROM POISONED STOP

He stopped there himself, wondering how to placate the super without either committing an inaccuracy or admitting to hunches. The truth, he decided:

CAUSE NOT YET KNOWN STOP MAXWELL OWINGS CHECK-
ING FOR POSSIBILITY OF SAME POTION AS CAUSED UL-
MANNS DEATH WILL ADVISE FURTHER SOON AS POSSIBLE
                                    MEDFORD

To Trehane he sent a series of requests—passport checks
on Elizabeth Smith, Catherine Elkin, and others. Dossiers
on the ship's officers.—Although, he thought, he might
as well have sent the passenger list and the names of the
entire ship's complement.

He then waited. It took the policeman an hour to arrive. And when finally there was a knock on his door, his
"Come in" brought two men. One was the policeman—unfortunately the same one. But Medford didn't have time
to soothe his feathers because Heinz, the lounge steward,
who was right behind him, said, "The captain's compliments, and would the Herr Inspektor please attend him in
the captain's cabin at the Herr Inspektor's earliest convenience?"

Medford stood up, and started to hand his cables to the
bobby, who said, "But one minute, please! *I* have a cable
for you." He glared at Heinz, who glared back.

Medford said, "Yes?"

The policeman found his very official envelope and
handed it over portentously.

Medford tore it open. The cable was signed by Trehane:

I HAVE A NILS SWENDSTROM TOO THAMES CHAP POSI-
TIVELY IDENTIFIED AS SUCH FROM FINGERPRINT STOP
MINE IS TERRENCE SWENDSTROM BEYOND QUESTION IS
YOURS COINCIDENCE QUERY MOST UNLIKELY STOP AM
CHECKING SHIPPING LINE HAMBURG ON SWENDSTROMS
APPOINTMENT AND ALSO LONDON AGENT WILL ADVISE
INSTANTER STOP IS YOUR SWENDSTROM STILL ALIVE

5

"A glorious day," the superintendent said sunnily.

Trehane blinked and crossed his elegant knees uneasily. "Yes, sir," he said. To himself, he said, *Always* agree, remember that, Trehane.

"Now"—the superintendent reverted to normal—"what is this nonsense, this request for a million men? Especially since you already have extra men?"

Trehane felt remotely relieved. One liked to know what one was agreeing with. He had asked for four detectives, and by the superintendent's lights that was a million men. And presumably his inheritance of Medford's Sergeant Brooks comprised the "extra men" he already had. He said, "Yes, sir. I mean, I have a great number of people to check on and—"

"And where have *you* been all day? Were you checking on people? What people? In what way have you been amusing yourself?"

"Well, I've been to a funeral"—that sounded a little too much like disagreement; he said hastily, "Barkland's funeral." That didn't help. "And"—he tried a change of subject—"I am off in a few minutes to meet Swendstrom's widow—lady presumed to be Swendstrom's widow—in the morgue."

"You've made your point: it hasn't been an amusing day. Well, has it been a profitable one? You must have *some* reason for wanting me to denude the section of all its men."

"Yes, sir. It's because of the funeral. There was a big turnout. Mostly patients. And a number of them had no file in Barkland's office. So they should be checked on."

"Ah. You think some chap took his file out of Barkland's office to conceal the fact that he was a patient, covered the omission by removing a fistful of others, and then showed happily up at the funeral to reveal that he knew Barkland?"

Trehane recrossed his knees. Put that way . . .

The superintendent performed one of the switches that so thoroughly unnerved Trehane. "I know," he said. "I understand. One has to try everything. But, please, let's try everything *else* first."

"Yes, sir." Trehane thought of the dozens of other facets he was pursuing in regard to his two corpses—his and Medford's, he thought; it really wasn't fair. "Well," he said, in agreement, "it's true that there is a good deal else to work on. Medford keeps *cabling.*"

"What would you like him to do? Use carrier pigeon?" And that was unfair, too.

"Well, carry on."

"Yes, sir."

Upon the fingerprint division's announcement that the print of a bit of forefinger turned over to them by the lab belonged to a man named Nils Swendstrom, M.D., and the file department's (unnecessary) report that a man named Nils Swendstrom had been one of those tried in connection with the Terrence Clinic abortions case (which Trehane, who had read the file carefully, well remembered)—upon such confirmation, Trehane, with admirable simplicity, had reached for a telephone directory. A Nils Swendstrom, M.D. was listed, at 12 B, Short Ridge Road, London, S.W. 6. He then contemplated the instrument itself, and decided that thoroughness, and perhaps delicacy, called for greater effort than it offered. Sergeant Brooks was forthwith dispatched to Fulham to see if there was a Mrs. Swendstrom, or suchlike.

Sergeant Brooks had telephoned in: There was indeed a Mrs. Swendstrom. Her husband was most fortuitously missing. She refused to leave until her two sons had come home from school and been fed. Then, that evening, at approximately seven-thirty, she would accompany Brooks to the morgue. Was that convenient? If so, would the inspector make sure that someone stayed late at the morgue?

"Yes, Brooks. Fine, thank you, Brooks," Trehane had said. "Not too difficult, I hope?"

"No sir. She 'ad 'ysterics, though."

She still had hysterics.

The morgue, Trehane thought (being different from Brooks only by virtue of a couple of generations of middle-class antecedents and a university education) was not a very cheerful place. And, too, the bits and pieces of Dr. Swendstrom weren't very appetizing.

They *were* the remains of Nils Swendstrom, however; Mrs. Swendstrom was certain of that.

Trehane found the identification mysterious (Trehane was a bachelor) but relieving. On the other hand, Mrs. Swendstrom's hysterics were unsettling.

She was plump, unpretty, unhappy, and Swedish-born, which led to sing-song speech and a peculiar set of vowels, all complicated by hysteria. Trehane tried coping in a gentlemanly way until he recalled the prescription for hysteria: a slap in the face. He said, "And may I ask, madam, why you did not report the absence of your husband?" Out of a corner of his eye he was astonished to see that the retiring Brooks actually gave an approving nod.

Mrs. Swendstrom indulged in one last sob, and then became impenetrably phlegmatic. It was an astonishing turn-about.

He tried for the other cheek: "It was a most suspicious lapse on your part."

"On my part? No, no. Because of my husband."

"What does that mean?"

"I didn't know what he might be doing."

"But it might have been something that he would prefer not to have the police be aware of?"

"How could I know?"

Now, there was an answer. But it provided a taking-off point. "Your husband still practiced medicine?"

"Ye-es."

"Yes or no?"

"Yes!"

"When he could? When he had a case to practice on?"

"What do you mean by that? He never touched a girl. Not since the trial."

"But he wasn't a very successful doctor?"

"Well, no. Not very."

"So how did he eke out a living?"

"Eek?"

"I beg of you not to start all that again. I *beg*—Oh. How did he *make* a living?"

"This way. That way."

"Which way and what way?"

It went on a long time, and it seemed to take more out of Trehane than Mrs. Swendstrom. She ended up fairly fresh and he ended up tired and not particularly enlightened. Mrs. Swendstrom probably did not really know what her husband's activities were composed of. But she suspected them. He did "odds and ends" and it was clear that she thought they were very odd indeed. But as to exactly what . . . On that she had only one idea, not very concrete, but helpful. She thought perhaps he extracted things out of Barkland.

"Things? You mean money?"

"Well, maybe a little money, but more often—things."

"What kind of things?"

"Recommendations. Things like that."

"Blackmail, Mrs. Swendstrom?"

"For why? Dr. Barkland was a friend, an old acquaintance."

"Dr. Barkland had apparently turned himself into a highly respectable, highly respected physician."

"So?"

That was answerable but probably not, he supposed, to a very new widow. He took the opposite tack, and it worked surprisingly well. Mrs. Swendstrom, he was beginning to realize, was stubborn and negative. She was inclined to take the negative tack on anything, and that trait could be turned to advantage. "On the other hand," Trehane murmured, as if to himself, "Dr. Barkland had taken no precautions to hide his past. So it would be hard to blackmail him."

"Not at all," said Mrs. Swendstrom promptly. "Maybe he didn't hide, but people didn't know. His patients didn't know, or maybe never heard of Terrence Clinic."

"Still . . ."

"You could get things out of him," she said complacently.

Well, at least he had learned how to deal with Mrs. Swendstrom. "So," he said, "you didn't report your husband's absence because you thought he might be doing something he shouldn't."

"No, no," said Mrs. Swendstrom with predictable contrariness. "He *told* me he might be going away."

"Ah, he did?"

"But"—negativeness, stubbornness, and battle departed suddenly and her face crumpled into what Trehane decided was her first moment of naturalness—"he didn't come home for his luggage. It's—still—standing—*there*." And she blubbered.

Trehane sighed, and signaled Brooks to take her away.

6

The captain rose, offered his hand, and waved at the seat across the desk from his own. He said, "How do you do?

I am sorry I was not here to welcome you." Those were form statements, routinely delivered, but the follow-up delivered with a cold passion: "And what has happened to my doctor?"

The best defense . . . Medford thought. "Poisoned," he said without loquacity, and smiled gently at the captain. A perfect Germanic type, but not the most common. A remnant of the Teutonic aristocracy, at the least the *niedere Adel* and perhaps even the *hohe Adel*—long-boned, with a long head, ice-blue eyes, and the long straight nose that perfectly fitted the face. Graying and balding though he now was, he had undoubtedly been a colorless blond; the facial tones confirmed it.

"Poisoned," the captain repeated, without inflexion, but Medford experienced a flash of insight. For all his assumption of Teutonic superiority the man was frightened. The captain said, "And what does that mean? Was the man fed hemlock? Did he eat something he shouldn't have, and he has a bellyache? Or has something gone wrong with the commissary? Can we all expect to be ill?" He added quickly, "In the last case, the fault lies with the home office. Most food is purchased there, and the kitchen staff is chosen there. Short of an actual mutiny in the kitchen, I have little to do with them." He looked faintly pleased, and that puzzled Medford. This was the sort of man who would normally wish to direct everything in sight; why did he seem pleased with a lack of authority? . . . The captain answered that question. He said, "So if the food is at fault, the blame lies with the home office, not with me." So, Medford thought, he was defensive about his job. Frightened for his job?

"Is it like the last doctor?"

"Ah, now." Medford shook his head. "It would seem to outrage coincidence to suggest that two doctors on the same ship could be poisoned at one-week intervals entirely without connection. But on the other hand, how can I know the answers? I was not present at the poisoning of the first doctor. What happened?"

"Happened? He was taken ill. He became unconscious. He vomited. He died. We were then without a doctor, of course, but one of the stewardesses is somewhat trained. She could find no heartbeat, no pulse, no breath. So I decided he was dead." From anyone else the conclusion could have been sarcasm; from the captain it was reportage. "*You* must tell *me* what happened. You must tell me why you are here. Why the home office saw fit to authorize your visit. Is the suggestion that Dr. Ulmann was murdered?"

"The doctor's death is simply considered difficult to understand, to explain away. For anyone to drink quantities of the preservative he consumed would be mysterious; for a doctor to do so is inexplicable. The authorities find it impossible to close their files. Without the suggestion having been made, the possibility of suicide is undoubtedly in their minds. Was Dr. Ulmann a suicidal type?" Of which there is probably no such thing, Medford added to himself.

But the captain took the term seriously and unhappily. After a minute's thought he shook his head and said with obvious reluctance, "No. He was a self-contained man. Cold. Hard. Self-seeking. Unsympathetic. And a heavy drinker."

A thumbnail sketch of the captain himself, Medford thought, resisting the inclination to sniff. The captain's comfortable cabin was redolent of fine cognac and equally strong, equally fine cigars.

"He was—grasping. I do not speak your language well, and I do not enjoy trying. So I will reduce my answer to the fact that suicide seems to me quite out of the question."

"Well, then, that leaves the possibilities of criminal neglect, and—"

"Neglect? Criminal neglect?" The captain had turned white.

"Quite. And the remoter possibility, which you raised: murder."

"And what about a mistake, a simple mistake on the part of the doctor himself?"

"Unlikely. The concoction has a taste."

"Well, then." The captain stood up. "You have until Monday. We will then sail. I have lost one day already because of Dr. Ulmann's death. I shall not lose another. So in the next two days, you must make up your mind as to the explanation behind Dr. Ulmann's death. Or abandon the quest."

There were other alternatives, Medford thought, as he unfolded himself out of his chair. If Swendstrom died the Italian authorities might refuse a sailing permit. And the shipping company itself might, as a result of Swendstrom's attack, order the ship to remain in Italy until the matter was cleared up. And even if the ship sailed, Medford did not necessarily have only two days, since he might sail with it.—God forbid, Medford thought, and said, "You will advise your officers and men to give me their co-operation?"

"Yes."

"And you will advise your home office of Dr. Swendstrom's illness, and of the other—casualties—you have aboard?"

"Other—" The captain broke off. He was almost as white as Swendstrom had been at Medford's first sight of the doctor. But despite the obvious anger, the captain retained a frigid and somewhat admirable dignity. He said, "It is not in your province to tell me what I should and should not do in regard to *my* ship and *my* principals. However, I shall assume you do not know better and answer: of course I shall advise them."

"Quite," Medford said mildly.

The captain had clearly had no intention of telling anyone anything until forced to it.

7

Trehane glanced at the clock and sighed. He was, or would like to have been, a man of regular habits, as befitted an Englishman, and an Englishman of his class. The time for a whisky was in the dim distance; the time for a civilized dinner was fairly remote. But his profession permitted no such propriety of time-recognition. He briefly contemplated his father's sanitary-fixtures manufacturing concern (which he was mistakenly certain his colleagues knew nothing of), shuddered, and settled deeper into his desk chair.

He glanced at the reports on the Terrence Clinic doctors' present and interim activities. The dossiers were filling in slowly. A longish business, that would be.

He checked on Medford's passport requests. Being followed up.

He checked on the ship's personnel report. Two had come in. He carefully read a short history of the purser and a longer one of the captain.

Unsavory characters. Germans. Captain seemed to have a most peculiar reputation. He put the papers aside for inclusion in his letter to Medford.

He picked up the typewritten dossier of Dr. Maxwell Owings, and the sight of it, plus lack of food, caused a slight heartburn to set in. *He* asked for a couple of extra men and the super blew up. But *Medford* asked for checks on everything short of the sinking of the *Lusitania* and the super said, "Why tell me? Get it for him." Most unfair.

Dr. Maxwell Owings' data had come in quickly (largely because the newspapers' files were freshly full of him). He had led an uneventful life. Medically full. One divorce. Wife remarried three years earlier; now in Phoenix, Arizona. No scandal. Altogether, almost none of the bits of scandal one usually came across when delving into a life. He had once beat up an interne; affair was dropped by both sides. That was little enough in the background of a man. Then there was the business of the Lloyd child. Being fair (and Trehane *was* fair; his great complaint against life was that no one else seemed to be)—being fair, the coldly written, factual report had the effect of supporting Medford's theory that the doctor had been guiltless. Put in this unemotional way, one could see that the whole thing might well have been blown up out of nothing.

Nothing in the report worth repeating to Medford, however. Except . . . Trehane considered, and then made a note for inclusion in his letter to Medford. To Trehane it meant nothing, but Medford was infamous for operating on a base of intuition, of random "connections." This was highly random, but it was a connection.

Well, then. Now he could write a letter and get out to find a bit of dinner. The letter would have to be written by hand since the shorthand-typists, luckier than he, had all departed long since.

There was a knock on his door, immediately followed by the entry of Sergeant Brooks, who marched to Trehane's desk and placed two sheets of paper on it.

Trehane said rhetorically, "And what have we here?"

Brooks had no sense of rhetoric. "From the superintendent, sir. Regarding attached communication."

"Thank you." Trehane was already well into the telegram. Then he said explosively, "Oh, my God!" It was an unusually heartfelt statement, and Brooks, equally unusually, responded to it; he said, "Yes, sir."

Perhaps if Trehane had known that he had echoed one of Medford's newest prayers, he would have felt a bit better. But he didn't know it.

He got up and started to pace the floor.

Brooks departed silently.

8

To Medford's knock, Owings called "Come in. Oh. Hello. This is Mr. Clarkson. Inspector Medford."

Mr. Clarkson had a healthy handshake to match his healthy physique and coloring.

Owings said, "Or is it 'Doctor'? The 'Reverend Mister'?"

"Plain 'mister' is fine." Clarkson beamed.

Owings was being helpful, Medford thought. He said to Owings, "How is your patient?"

"Emptied. As hollow as an ancient oak."

"Which is good?"

"Which is the only possible treatment. And if we caught it early enough it is good. No one seems to know when the doctor was taken ill. Last seen quite a while after lunch. So perhaps we caught it early enough, which is good. So, we wait. The stewardess is standing by. She'll call me if necessary. And your suggestion was exactly right. He was full of the stuff. Plus quantities of alcohol." He looked up at Medford curiously. "How on earth did you peg that?"

"Sort of a long story."

"Untellable, huh?" Owings had a pleasant grin.

Medford said, "And your other patients?"

"Miss Smith hasn't come out of her retirement. I'm going to drop around first thing in the morning. Mr. Clarkson has very kindly been sitting with Miss Elkin. He says she's feeling fine. I'll drop in after dinner." He sighed. "This trip was supposed to be a sort of vacation before I take over a very exacting post in Hong Kong. But I might as well be in residence. As for dinner, it's so late if I don't get down I won't get any at all. Will you join Clarkson and me for some dinner?"

Medford shook his head. "Thanks, but I've arranged for a sandwich in my room. I've finally been given a cabin, just two doors down." He gestured forward. "So I'll go, unpack my extra shirt, and do some paper work. I want to get an early start in the morning. Frankly, I'd like to get back to London as soon as possible."

"Advisable." Clarkson nodded emphatically. "Ship is getting entirely out of hand. Like a bordello on the madam's day out."

Medford had only a lightweight dressing gown. He had thought of Genoa as being south and sunny. The night was thick with a gaseous fog that was curling evilly through his fractionally opened porthole. Might as well be in London, he thought, and scratched out the last sentence in his umpteenth attempt. He then wrote: "Ship is—" He paused, smiled. "—like a bordello on the madam's day out" was not the superintendent's form of humor. It was a damned odd simile coming from a clergyman, Devonshire by origin, if Medford's usually good ear was in working order. Ah, well.

He leaned forward again and wrote firmly. Then he made a copy of the result, burned the attempts in the ash tray, and sat back to read the final achievement.

MY SWENDSTROM STILL ALIVE BUT NO CONDITION FOR QUESTIONING STOP OWINGS SAYS IT IS TOUCH AND GO STOP POISON IDENTIFIED AS SAME AS THAT WHICH KILLED ULMANN STOP SHIP IS IN STATE OF CONFUSION ONE WOMAN AMNESIAC ANOTHER ATTACKED PHYSICALLY STOP HENCE MY QUESTIONS REGARDING PASSPORTS

Then he sat back again, cleared his mind, and prepared to make some of the "assumptions" that so annoyed the superintendent initially, the results of which so often gratified him.

One, fact: The ship's Swendstrom was not Swendstrom. Reason: That fingerprint. So who *was* this Swendstrom?

Assumption: Possibly the murderer of the real Swendstrom. Reason: When a man masquerades as a murdered man, it is not illogical to suspect he may have killed him. Not too strong, that one, but further: The dead Swendstrom was not immediately identified, but the ship's Swendstrom must have known he was dead or he would not have risked the masquerade, which meant at least that he had knowledge of the murder. Further: He had papers that must have been taken off the dead Swendstrom. . . .

Medford stumbled suddenly over a hole in his knowledge: When did the Thames Swendstrom die? The man had been in the water, he had been badly eaten away, but some estimate must have been possible from the examination of the internal organs. Medford realized with a tinge of shock that he had not so much as seen the autopsy report. The omission seemed quite unforgivable on his part, but as he thought about it he saw the reason: The superintendent had been so triumphant about his "link"—the bullet—that they had both quite forgotten normal procedure. Well, his first question to Trehane was therefore a simple one. He picked up his pencil and wrote:

WHEN DID THAMES SWENDSTROM DIE
ACCORDING TO AUTOPSY REPORT QUERY

He sat back.

Now, if the ship's Swendstrom had killed the Thames' Swendstrom . . . But Medford had suggested to the super that the murderer of Barkland was probably the unwilling murderer of the real Swendstrom. So was the ship's Swendstrom also the murderer of Barkland? Medford decided that at this stage he could only say, Possibly.

The reply to "Who was the ship's Swendstrom" was not so far even a beginning of an answer. Medford had assumed *deeds* on the part of the ship's Swendstrom, but had not tackled the question of *who* he was. So . . .

The Terrence Clinic affair, which Medford had mentioned to the super as being "in the background," had now moved to the foreground. Both doctors, Swendstrom and

Barkland had been involved in it. How about the ship's Swendstrom? *Was* he a doctor? Something in Owings' attitude, something indefinable, suggested that Owings might not consider Swendstrom a licensed doctor. But . . . there had been a medical *student* involved in the Terrence Clinic affair, *and*—Medford felt the small thumping sensation that successful (if leaping) assumptions usually brought him—*and* the medical student had been named Gonzales. He thought happily of the Latin appearance of the sick man in the doctor's cabin. In addition, that affair had taken place ten years before; this man looked to be in the neighborhood of thirty. So the age fit. He picked up his pen and wrote:

HAVE YOU COMPLETED CHECK ON TERRENCE CLINIC STUDENT ROBERTO GONZALES QUERY SERVED SIX MONTHS WHAT HAPPENED TO HIM UPON RELEASE STOP

Where now? Well, how about that business of Barkland being the prime murderee, Swendstrom the accidental one. In that case, the ship's Swendstrom would have killed Barkland for reasons as yet impossible to guess at, been happened in on by Swendstrom, killed him to prevent his being a witness, and then stolen his identity to get away with. Perhaps; it was so far unprovable and terribly far from being watertight.

However, if one took seriously Dr. Owings' report—stopped worrying about Owings' reluctance, motives, etc.—accepted that the ship's doctor had tried to kill, or at least wound, the Smith girl—then motives began to form foggily. The name Clarkson caused her fright, she had reported to Owings. Clarkson—Barkland? And Swendstrom "frightened" her.—Medford shook his head: later; it was much too obscure now. But it did lead to a checkable point. He added his third question:

WHEN WAS ELIZABETH SMITHS TICKET PURCHASED QUERY PLEASE CHECK ON ALL TICKETS OF THOSE WHO BOARDED AT SOUTHAMPTON STOP

135

He reflected unhappily that there was a huge flaw in all this. He was going along assuming that the ship's Swendstrom was Gonzales, and a murderer and villain, but to do so was to ignore the fact that the Latinish gentleman below decks had himself been poisoned, was currently a victim rather than a villain. To that Medford had a weak but possible answer, the answer he had given the superintendent: If there was a multiplicity of involvements here, possibly the ship's Swendstrom was the villain of one set of events, the victim of another.

What other? The death of Ulmann? No. The Latinish Swendstrom hadn't been aboard, and if one was to assume that he had any form of complicity in Dr. Ulmann's death one would then have to assume that if he murdered the real Swendstrom it had not been by accident.

Something is missing, Medford thought. He examined the thought, decided it would have sounded foolish if uttered aloud . . . so *much* was missing. But I mean a big thing, he told himself. There is something big that we don't even suspect. Something, something.

That "something" was defeating him. But it would come (Medford had a profound belief that crime did not pay), it would come. There was nothing to do but wait.

And Miss Elkin? Well, Miss Elkin's case was clear. The "assumptions" weren't even that; they were facts. At the moment, however—

To the knock, Medford said, "Come in," and rose as his outraged messenger boy marched militarily into the cabin.

Medford sighed and put himself to the task of being charming. "Will you have a drink, Sergeant?" he asked. It was the oldest ploy in the world, but what with all the braid the bobby was wearing it *could* have been possible that Medford didn't know the difference.

SUNDAY

```
SUNDAY    20TH JANUARY    GENUA
                §
Religious Services will be held in the
     dining room at ten o'clock.
                §
We remind that the Upper-boatsdeck is
     reserved for adults only.
                §
To go ashore passengers must have a
LANDING CARD.  LANDING CARDS are available
at the Purser's Büro (open from 10.00—
noon, 4.00—6.00 p.m.)
                §
Passengers making shore trips are here
reminded that the  M.S. TILBURG will
sail for Port Saïd at approximately 5.00
p.m. on Monday, 21st January.
```

"Good morning," Max said. He nodded at the notice. "I'm not used to seeing anything posted so early."

The purser shrugged and then winced. "*Gut* morning,"

he said, and Max realized that it was a polite lie; the morning was unspeakable for the purser, who was suffering from what Max diagnosed as a hangover, and a giant of its type. His normally pale face was now pale yellow, and what was visible of his eyes was deep saffron. "Ships' runs are of course reported from noon to noon, but when we are in port I am always glad to keep well advised the passengers." He winced again.

Max felt sympathy. He could think of few maladies (including the common cold) more miserable than the common hangover. He said, "Religious service? What kind?"

"Whatever kind Mr. Clarkson dispenses."

"I see . . . Look, will you permit me to give you something for your—ah—indisposition?"

The dull yellow face took on an orange tint—red mixed with the yellow, Max decided. The purser said, "Ah, that would be—helpful." He suffered a seizure, probably of nausea, downed it, and said in a rush, "It would be most gracious. There is a cure?"

"That is the unanswered prayer of several million people. However, there are alleviations. Come along to my cabin."

Medford faced the day of rest with a grim determination to do no such thing.

His ruminations—"assumptions"—of the night before seemed, by the dim Genoese daylight, extremely murky. For the first time in his life he was experiencing the emotion that more orthodox policemen knew well—a fervent wish for rules and regulations. At least he would like to know *what* he was investigating.

Not being very sure about that, he would have to try to behave like a proper policeman, deal with first things first, ignore the amorphous, anomalous quality of the business, try to forget that there was no fitness, no order, no beginning—and, it began to seem, possibly no end.

In line with his new acceptance of the first-things-first rule he had gone, as early as seemed possible, to visit the ship's Swendstrom. Her charge was much better, said the stewardess who, with German thoroughness, had bedded herself down in the doctor's small cabin and was still in residence. Medford had enticed her into the corridor and she there became the first of his interviewees (whom he had listed on a slip of paper). Questioned about Ulmann, she acknowledged that she had been in attendance on that gentleman when he died, but she added nothing to Medford's facts. The attack had been much like the one Dr. Swendstrom suffered. Dr. Ulmann had said nothing; he was found in his bed in the morning and had died a little after seven that evening without regaining full consciousness.

Medford thanked her and went to the upper deck, checking his list en route: The seaman who had found Miss Elkin, and then the bartender.

In a main-deck corridor he met Owings, who said, " 'Morning. Getting your early start?"

"A policeman's lot . . ."

"*And* a doctor's. I have a new patient."

"For God's sake not—"

"No, no. Just an advanced case of galloping hangover. Purser. Just dosed him and sent him to bed."

"Oh. Damn. I was en route to ask his co-operation."

"There are assistant pursers."

"Yes, of course. Hadn't thought of that. So, off on our rounds, huh?"

"Our 'antic round.'"

" 'Light fantastic round.' Milton for Shakespeare."

Owings smiled. "Bet I can stop you: 'Our appointed rounds.'"

Medford pondered it. Then he said, "Stopped. Who's that?"

"Unfair. U. S. Government mailmen. I'll turn you into an American yet." He waved and went down the corridor.

Not if the superintendent knew anything about it, Medford thought, and smiled. He liked Owings.

"Sit down, please," Elizabeth Smith said. "I'd like to talk to you."

"What else am I here for?" Owings smiled, but inwardly he had tensed. This unsarcastic calmness, this level, pleasant, normal-register voice seemed to come from a new personality, a third one.

"I am a Californian," she said abruptly, and then paused, sorting out. She was far better-looking today. She had dressed in black, which seemed neither too young nor too old, and her hair was brushed off her forehead most becomingly. Owings revised his phraseology: she was beautiful. "I was an orphan. I can remember most of my childhood. As much as is probably usual. When I was eight my parents died in an accident and I went to live with my grandfather, my mother's father. He was elderly even then. He didn't marry until he was almost fifty, and my mother had been his only child. I remember all about him, and the house in Glendale, and school. I entered the University of Southern California when I was seventeen and when I was a little over eighteen my grandfather died." She stopped.

Max said gently, "And?"

"Nothing. I just stop there. I've been thinking about this since I woke up at three this morning and said to myself, 'Now, Beth, turn over and go back to sleep.' I am called 'Beth.' And my name *is* Smith." She paused again. "From three this morning until now, for over six hours, I have been remembering detail by detail, and yet I stop at my eighteenth year." Her eyes came back from the past and fastened on him. They were level and very appealing. "That isn't right, is it? People don't remember like that, do they? Either they remember everything, or splashy bits. Not just half of a life?"

"Of course they do," Max lied. It was damned peculiar. But, after all, there were few rules in amnesia. "There are few rules," he said more truthfully. "What sort of things do you remember?"

"That's interesting." She spoke slowly. "I have a feeling

140

that I am not only remembering, but that I am re-evaluating. For instance, I think I admired, respected, and feared my grandfather. But it occurs to me now—and, as I say, I think this is new—that he was a stuffy, dirty-minded despot. I think he expected me to—to 'go wrong,' as they said in Victorian novels, and that he spent all his time flattening me, frightening me, reducing me as to personality and appearance. I think he wanted me to be unattractive, uninteresting, uninviting." She looked up at Max with an air of bewilderment. "I *think*," she repeated. "But perhaps I am being unfair. Or self-centered."

" 'Self-centered,' " Max said, "sounds like grandfather."

"Yes! Exactly! That's just what I meant. If I had a thought about how to fix my hair, or repeated a compliment, I was told I was self-centered. I think I became abnormally self-*un*interested. If there is such a word."

"I understand what you mean. You know," Max said gently, "such a situation is not unusual." And it possibly accounted for her present multiple personalities. The meek little lamb was grandfather's girl. And the others? Well, perhaps the sophisticated, sarcastic woman was the revolt against grandfather. And—happily supposing—the level-headed charmer of this moment was either what had evolved from the center of the two, or might now evolve.

He spent an hour with her, listening patiently. She didn't seem to try very hard to get beyond her eighteenth year, but she was fascinated by her ability to recall the minutiae of events that lay behind that birthday. It was a sad record of everyday nothings, pathetically revealing itself as a fantastically uneventful life, more suited to seventy than to seventeen.

Max listened.

Medford spent his minute of waiting gazing at the empty pool's bottom through the heavy meshes of rope. Then the deckhand whom he had asked to see arrived.

The deckhand's name was Willy. He was an enormous lad of twenty, well educated, intelligent. This was a between-university-courses trip for him. He made an excellent witness, even speaking enough English to be intelligible to Medford, who had a smattering of Italian but whose German was limited to *Danke schön*.

And all the boy's helpful clarity didn't help a bit. He had heard a scream. It was immediately followed by a thump. Each sound was extremely vivid. The scream sounded like a woman; the thump sounded as if she had hit the bottom of the pool. He had run to the pool, rushed down, and lifted the woman's head. But when he saw the blood, he desisted.

Medford blinked slightly over "desisted" and then nodded.

"So I see a steward, I send him for Doktor, he bring Doktor." The boy spread his hands as a period of finality.

"I see. And the net"—Medford put out a toe and touched the heavy rope—"why wasn't it in place? Surely it wasn't warm enough for swimming?"

"*Ach, nein. Freitag.*"

"Friday?"

"*Ja. Wöchentlich—einmal wöchentlich*"—the boy struggled and then said in a rush—"all the Fridays we polish."

Just German thoroughness. Medford sighed.

The bartender was a very different type from the deckhand—twice his age, half his size, far more sophisticated, probably less intelligent. While the deckhand was a gentleman, the bartender was a servant. His English was excellent, his manner subservient. Also, he was evasive. After rephrasing his question several times, Medford decided that the evasiveness was a bartender's habit rather than deliberate avoidance. Medford countered with bluntness: "Let me put it this way: who aboard drinks?"

"Many aboard take aperitifs. The elderly English gentleman with the cane, Cabin Twelve—"

"I mean the staff, not the passengers. And I mean drinks to excess, not sips aperitifs."

"The staff? The officers are not permitted to drink to, ah, excess."

"Now, look," Medford said firmly, "haven't you been told to co-operate with me?"

"Yes, but—"

"There are no buts. And we are not going to quibble over definitions. The captain—let us take the captain. He drinks cognac, no?"

Inexplicably, the bartender brightened. "Yes, sir." The thin dark head nodded emphatically.

"Quantities of it?"

"Yes, sir!"

"What about the others?"

"Well, the chief engineer drinks, but only occasionally. He goes on—that is . . . occasionally. Last Wednesday night, for instance, he spent the late evening here with the German miss, Fräulein Gotthelf. They—he drank a great deal." He paused, apparently couldn't resist it, and added, "They both did."

So, Medford thought, despite his initial caution the bartender, like so many of his kind, was a gossip. "So the captain drinks in his cabin, the chief engineer drinks a great deal but only on occasions. And the others?"

"That's all." He sounded wistful.

"How about Dr. Ulmann?"

"Ah, but I thought you meant the present staff! Dr. Ulmann was a very, very heavy drinker."

"Did he become morose? Unhappy?"

"No, he became gay. Very good fun."

Damn. "And of the present staff, how about Dr. Swendstrom?"

"He has been in here only once. He drank orange juice."

So he couldn't even consider writing Ulmann off as a possible "Suicide while intoxicated." And there was no apparent connection between the fact that the two doctors had been drinking alcohol before their attacks since drinking was usual for Ulmann, probably unusual for Swendstrom. He said grimly, "Thanks."

In the lounge off the bar, he thought, Off on my appointed rounds, was reminded of Owings' morning, and turned back into the bar. "The purser," he said. "What about the purser?"

The bartender looked up, surprised. "Why, nothing," he said. "Herr Herbst buys a couple of bottles of spirits—usually cognac—once every several months. He never drinks in here, and I've only seen him show any sign of having drunk anything at all once or twice in the four years I've been aboard. I imagine he has a small drink before dinner. Perhaps before bed. Something like that."

"Um. Thanks again."

"Come in." Miss Elkin's voice was weak but cheerful.

Medford entered, and found that Clarkson was sitting beside the bed. He had the comfortable look of a man settling in for the duration. Clarkson said, "*Good* morning!"

"Good morning." Medford bowed to Miss Elkin who, although innocent of anything resembling make-up, and with her thin hair yanked severely upward, was sporting a quilted bed jacket covered with yellow roses and green sprigs. The thing was extremely pretty, Medford thought, and the old gal looked like a nice duck.

She said, "It's Inspector Medford, isn't it? Have I got that right? I'm afraid I was a wee bit woozy when you dropped in yesterday."

"Indeed you were. That's why I dropped out."

She had a very nice laugh. It was musical, as was her speaking voice. Medford also discovered that he felt rather witty. Miss Elkin said, "But now I am *quite* recovered. Dr. Owings is being kind, giving me an unusual and unnecessary day in bed, and Mr. Clarkson pretends he is company but I think he is actually a watchdog."

"Against a further attack?"

"Attack! My goodness, no! I meant that Mr. Clarkson was seeing to it that I remain in bed. Attack! Was it an attack? On *me?*"

"We must discuss that, musn't we?" Medford looked at Clarkson, who seemed entrenched as if for life. Medford said, "I thought you were conducting a service this morning, Mr. Clarkson?"

"Was, and did." But Clarkson unfastened himself from the chair. "Thirty minutes seemed quite enough. I really don't know them well enough to discuss the various sins, and besides, *I* always hate to be bored. I think perhaps"—he moved easily toward the door—"that I escaped *that* sin. After the ceremony one of our mutual countrymen—handsome old type who walks with a cane—arthritis, I think—said, 'That was a nice travelogue, sir.' I've been pondering what I *should* have replied ever since."

Medford felt remotely fascinated. "May I ask, sir—what did you *actually* say?"

"Oh, just that it had seemed advisable to talk of Sarawak, which I know well indeed, since I know absolutely nothing, at first hand, of either heaven or hell."

Medford looked to see if he could laugh, found he could, and did. Then, inexplicably, he changed his mind. "Why don't you stay, Mr. Clarkson? If you have time?"

Clarkson turned promptly and took the chair near the door. "With alacrity, as the saying goes. I thought you wanted to grill the suspect in privacy."

"Ah, but Miss Elkin is not the suspect, is she?"

"Um," said Clarkson.

Medford took the chair Clarkson had vacated. He looked into Miss Elkin's eyes—pale blue, without any particular beauty but of a fine clarity—and said, "What happened, Miss Elkin?"

Her eyes left his face and fastened on her ringless hands. She said, her charming voice muted, "Do you know, I just can't remember."

Miss Elkin seemed usually to have an inner quality that Medford couldn't define—it was like a shimmer of warmth, a muted radiance. At the moment it was quite gone. "I see," he said. "Well, thank you."

There was a clammy silence in the room. Medford stood

up, nodded at Miss Elkin, said, "Well," and to Clarkson, "See you at lunch?"

"Shortly," Clarkson said shortly. He, too, seemed sadly dimmed.

2

Medford asked the chief steward if he could sit at Dr. Owings' table and was told that it was entirely convenient since the purser was "too busy to lunch."

The first thing to meet his gaze was an expansive black eye. Oh, my God, thought Medford, and was introduced to the eye's owner, a tiny Japanese with the unbelievable name of Mrs. Pitkethly. Admirably, she made no mention of and no excuse for her eye. Mr. Pitkethly was twice her size and of a type that Medford disliked vastly.

Medford had worked his way through Räucheraal (which turned out to be smoked eel), Salzgurke (salted cucumbers), antipasto (antipasto), Doppelte Kraftbrühe (double consommé) and was in the waiting period, joining Mrs. Pitkethly in watching Mr. Pitkethly eat an enormous portion of strawberry ice cream, when Max Owings arrived. Owings said, "Hi. What's good?" He looked tired.

"The smoked eel is excellent," Medford said promptly, "the cucumbers are devilish salty, the antipasto is anti-Italian, and the double consommé is less than single. But the surprise quality is delightful. I am now awaiting Set-zei-er mit Ni-er-en.—I *do* know that 'mit' means 'with.' "

Owings smiled and looked less tired. "Fried eggs with kidneys, and very good aboard—if you don't have a prejudice against kidneys."

"Practically our English national dish, and we English don't have prejudices anyway; we have convictions."

"Stand corrected. I will admit the German language taints the food for me at times. Mr. Pitkethly, for instance, is eating Erdbeer-Rahmeis."

"My God," Medford said. "That's strawberry ice cream?"

Pitkethly looked up briefly, smiled falsely, nodded, and returned to his ice cream.

"You speak German?" Medford said to Owings.

"High-school variety. Seems to work with menus, but not much further." He tackled smoked eel, Medford faced his eggs and kidneys, and the Pitkethlys bowed themselves away.

Medford said, "You bothered by talking while eating?"

"Only time a doctor gets to talk. Especially on the *Tilburg*."

"Then, a few questions?"

"Sure."

"Will you repeat your initial discussion with Miss Elkin and your impressions of her?"

Max looked up at him out of the corner of a curious eye. "That won't be conversation. That'll be a monologue. Oh, well"—and he repeated the detailed story of his first evening at the table with Miss Elkin.

When he had finished Medford nodded silently and attended to his plate. After several bites of Nieren he said, "So when I came aboard yesterday and you were being a bit antagonistic— It's all right," he added, as Max opened his mouth, "but you were rather, you know. I suspect it was because you like Miss Elkin and were angry on her behalf?"

"Yes," Max said. "Exactly."

"I see." Medford attended to his plate for another minute and then looked up abruptly. "And that," he demanded, "was also the reason for your fib-by-implication? I noticed your attitude and asked if you found it odd that Miss Elkin couldn't remember what had happened to her, and you replied that, 'medically speaking,' it was not odd. But you were recalling that she possesses a phenomenal memory."

Max looked disconcerted. Then he laughed. "So detectives *do* detect! I've always wondered."

"I'm right?"

"You are."

"And so it means that in some way, to some degree, Miss Elkin is involved."

"That is simply out of the question."

"Don't get antagonistic again. To a degree, a small degree, I'll admit, she is lying. And Mr. Clarkson had sadly noted that fact too. I just left him at her bedside, all his humor toned down from blue to muddiness. So three of us don't believe her." He munched on Setzeier.

Max looked mutinous.

Medford eyed him. "Shall I tell you why I think she's lying? And what the lie is?"

"My, my," Max said sarcastically. "You can do all that?"

"Let's see if you agree. Fact: Miss Elkin told you she had an excellent memory. Now she says she has forgotten. Not very conclusive, but a possible nail in the coffin of her honesty. Second fact: She added that all her senses were unusually acute. Right?"

"Yes."

"Well, now, she was hit from the rear, so she probably didn't see anything. It is unlikely that she heard anything identifiable although if we had an asthmatic case aboard I would give him some thought. Being hit in that way wouldn't give her a chance in a million to grapple with her assailant, so we can probably dismiss the idea that she touched something—a recognizable tweed, for instance, such as Mr. Clarkson wears, or the distinctive feeling of braid, like the captain's tortured cuffs or the doctor's caduceus. Now, what does that leave?"

"Nothing. As far as I can see, you have just brilliantly destroyed your whole proposition."

"Smell, doctor. Her sense of smell."

"Oh." Max looked surprised and then alert. "The captain?" he said. "He smells like an old-fashioned saloon, upper-class type."

148

"Possibly. Or Dr. Swendstrom. The cologne you mentioned."

"And speaking of cologne, there's Fräulein Gotthelf."

So Owings was still unwilling to have a hand in a conscious attack on the ship's doctor. "Who," Medford asked, "is Fräulein Gotthelf?"

"You haven't met her? Well, you will, you will. She's a lady who stinks. Anyway"—stubbornness resettled on Max's face—"*why?* Why should anyone want to conk Miss Elkin? Don't detectives look for reasons? Motives?"

"They do indeed. Your oral report supplied it. You don't remember?"

"Remember what?"

"Miss Elkin told you someone aboard was 'incognito.'"

"By God, she did!" Max stared at him. "She did!"

"So."

"Someone doesn't want to be identified?"

"It's a possible explanation."

Max sipped coffee reflectively. Then he said, "There's a flaw."

"Yes?"

"No matter what you say, Miss Elkin is no liar. If she thinks she knows who hit her, why should she lie? Why should she even evade?"

"Perhaps because, not being at all stupid, she realizes her danger."

"No," Max said positively. "She is a brave woman."

Medford shrugged and dismissed the matter. He asked, "Your first patient, Miss Smith. How is she?"

"Switch in the grilling, huh? She's a little better."

"Remembering?"

"Yes, a little. Nothing conclusive. But the fog should clear now, if only bit by bit."

"How about her? Is she honest? Is she lying?"

Max took a long time about answering, and when he did his voice was slow: "I don't think she's lying."

"But you wouldn't care to take an oath on it?"

"Amnesia is tricky. I just don't know."

"The thing that intrigues me is the empty front page in her passport."

Max looked at him sharply. "Detectives do detect," he repeated, but without the laughter. "I noticed that too."

Medford shrugged. "London has the passport number. They'll go through the U. S. Embassy to the New York passport bureau. There, filled out in the handwriting of the applicant, is the form that will tell us all about the possessor, place and date of birth, height, weight, age, color of eyes, names of parents, and so forth, and so forth."

Max looked startled. "Why, of course. I should have done that, shouldn't I? Should have asked the captain, or cabled New York myself. Or something."

"Little difference. Because even with the weight of the Yard behind the questions the answers will take quite a time in coming. Cables are all very well, but several people will be involved. Time-taking."

"You did the same thing—made the same passport request—about a number of people, I take it?"

"Quite." Medford smiled. "You *are* Maxwell Owings?"

Max grinned back at him. "It's all I'm prepared to admit." His grin faded and grimness replaced it. He added, "A lot of other people know me too."

There was a small silence and then Medford said, "The British are very reticent, you know, so I must uphold the national trait and not ask if you're referring to that non-sense about the Lloyd child."

"Thank you for 'nonsense.'"

"I was being entirely honest, and I should imagine that a very great number of people agree with me. If you'll permit me to phrase it as I, and a number of others must think of it: You were asked by an understandably emotional mother to travel to a remote village in Wales. Instead of ignoring the request—famous specialists must get a number of such—you went quite far: you investigated, got reports from the child's doctors, were told by them that the case could not be in any way helped by your special techniques, examined their reports in support of their opinions, and agreed. So you did not travel to the remote village."

"You read *The Times*. That's an expansion of my explanation."

"And a lot of people read the Flash's outpourings. But a number of them do it for sheer amusement. They put no faith in that scandal sheet."

"Well, thanks." Owings looked both stiff and relieved. Medford thought that the trial by cheap journalism would have been difficult for anyone, but more so for Owings. In some ways he was unusually sensitive.

Owings proceeded to be mildly insensitive. "Changing the subject," he said, "and reverting to your detecting abilities, which I've been praising for the past fifteen minutes, how do you feel about Dr. Swendstrom now?"

"Feel? Oh." Medford smiled. "Everything I said—or my interpretation of everything *you* said—still applies."

"So he poisoned himself thoroughly to confuse us?"

"Maybe he didn't know how thorough a job he was doing."

"As a doctor, one would think—" But Owings interrupted himself. "That reminds me. Out of a most unclear sky you suddenly announced that you could offer me assurance—which I hadn't asked for—that Swendstrom is a qualified physician—and in marched Heinz to tell us that, doctor or not, he was dead or dying. How did you—" This time he was interrupted. He looked up at the splendidly uniformed man who was waiting for him to be quiet so that he could speak.

Medford said, "My lovely aide. . . . *Buon giorno*." He accepted an elaborately sealed envelope.

Max stood up. "Off on my frantic rounds," he said.

3

Medford sat in the Winter Garden, a glassed-in room forward on the main deck. At the moment its name seemed rather too appropriate. A weak sun playing on the forbidding dockside walls did nothing to improve the look of Genoa from this angle. But the very dreariness of the room succeeded in keeping it empty, and that was an advantage. Medford had been sitting there, alone and almost motionless, for two hours.

On his knee lay a pad and pencil, and on top of the pad was Trehane's long handwritten letter. Medford read it for the seventh time:

Dear Medford,
    I'll try to take matters one at a time.
    Passports: No replies yet. Will push.
    People your end: Enclosed a dossier of captain, and some bare facts on purser. Rest of personnel information by tomorrow. So far, only surprising titbit in personal backgrounds is that Maxwell Owings started medical life as a psychoanalyst. Later returned to training and took up neurosurgery. The super would disapprove of my bothering to report that—"part of the subterranean canal that has nothing to do with the river we are supposed to be following"—but I know how you work, and Barkland was a psychoanalyst. (?) Otherwise Owings' background shows no surprises. Was a mediocre student until respecialization; then considered brilliant. Married sixteen years ago; divorced thirteen years ago. Ex-wife remarried three years ago, now Mrs. John T. (Juliette) Borden of Phoenix, Arizona. He's had no brushes with

152

police, although he once attacked, rather severely, an interne. Almost eight years ago. (Owings had had operation for deviated septum, interne implied reason was vanity.) Matter did not come to court.

Barkland: Funeral really astonishing. For a man without family, amazing turnout. Seems to have been revered, almost worshiped. Confessional type, of course, but still amazing. Many patients attended funeral whose files were missing from his office—really too many to check on. And who's to say that the pertinent one did show up? Odds against it, actually.

Swendstrom: Ours is unquestionably Nils Swendstrom, M.D., of the Terrence Clinic trials. Remnants identified by wife. She is Swedish born (he was born in Manchester) and not too intelligent. However, after her hysteria died down she was willing to talk. Knows just enough to be tantalizing. Swendstrom emerges as a ne'er-do-well, no practice to speak of. Eked things out in ways she suspected were, at the least, shady. She can't explain what they were, but among them she thinks was blackmail. She doesn't call it that—suggests that he had "friends." I gather that Barkland was among these donating "friends" and that he occasionally helped Swendstrom out in one way or another. Not too clear, I'll admit; merely one of the foggy bits.

London office of shipping line: Conway's in Bond Street know nothing about Swendstrom beyond fact that, as per request from the Hamburg office, they opened unusually early last Monday morning in order to turn over money, ticket to Southampton, and official papers to a Dr. Swendstrom. All their instructions on the matter came from the home office and they resist the suggestion that there was anything abnormal about that. They are purely a passenger office, they emphasize; have nothing whatever to do with scheduling, staffing, or running of the ships. Two of your intangibles came out of my interview with them: one, they do not usually receive instructions from the secretary of the line himself. He is a high official, too important to handle details. This is somewhat outweighed by the fact that the death of Ulmann could be considered an unusual emergency.

Second: the girl who dealt with "Swendstrom" (?) remembers him, with a bit of bridling, because she says he
was movie-star handsome. (?)

Yours,

Trehane's signature was as curlicue as "Swendstrom's"
dancing was reported to be.

Medford resisted the temptation to count the question
marks in the letter; instead he read once more the fairly
astounding postscript (Trehane's flowing handwriting had
tightened up a bit on that P. S., as if he were himself over-
come by cramps—a not unlikely possibility, Medford
thought):

A cable just received from Hamburg office shipping
line reports cable received by them from Interpol advising that the M. S. *Tilburg* and two other ships of same
line are almost certainly delivering crude opium from
port of Hong Kong (also some purchased in Singapore)
to ports of Southampton, Rotterdam, and Hamburg.
Checked Dangerous Drugs Department of Home Office
which advises same information from Interpol received
by them this morning. Does it tie in? Please advise.

That last question mark was going too far, Medford considered with a touch of warmth. "Does it tie in?" indeed.
He reverted to his new incantation: What the devil? He
recalled Owings' comment on the *Tilburg*'s Maugham-ish
quality. But opium was carrying the thing too far.

But . . . suppose it was the missing link, the "something" Medford had felt was missing? The other set of
events? He experienced a happy little thump, and then
gave in to a two-hour temptation.

Upon the first reading of Trehane's letter, he had tried
dealing with first things first: over two hours before he had
trotted up to the captain's cabin like a good little detective.

To the question, Did he know his ship was suspected of
transporting opium into Europe? the captain had reacted
with an astonishing display of opposites. He went from

open-mouthed speechlessness to verbal pyrotechnics, from dumb wonder to indignant denials, from outraged protest to pathetic plea.

Medford had come away suspecting that the captain was probably entirely aware, if not of opium-smuggling, at least that something irregular was going on aboard his ship. To Medford, the biography enclosed in Trehane's letter supplied the probable answer to the riddle of the captain: the man lived under a cloud he had no hope of dispelling. He wanted to retain his command for the necessary length of time—i.e., until pension time—without experiencing any cloudbursts. On the other hand, he might be smuggling opium. (And he might have attacked Miss Elkin. Owings was quite right in that the combination of black cigars and up-tilted cognac bottles had endowed the captain with a distinctive odor.)

So "first things first" as the superintendent used the phrase was of no use when it meant questioning the captain. But "first things first" in Medford's lexicon meant something quite else: shape the crime, the events, in your mind; find a possible starting place, or joining place; from that point fit in, or try to fit in, the rest of the details. With such a system, when one went wrong he went terribly wrong, and then to explain how he had arrived at so inept an end was almost impossible. But it was Medford's way and, however dangerous, he would stick to it.

If one made the assumption (not aloud; not for the super's benefit) that opium smuggling, being the most heinous of crimes, the most profitable, and one of the most dangerous, was the missing "something," a number of things fitted in.

Opium smuggling gave the affair a duration, a continuing-time aspect. One no longer thought of matters as dating from the moment of Ulmann's death.

(On the blank sheet of paper lying on his knee he noted a question he would ask of the captain.)

And so, if opium smuggling was the missing "something," the starting point was the whole ship, its crew, and—he looked back at Trehane's postscript: "the M. S. *Tilburg* and two other ships of same line"—and the starting point was also the whole shipping line's staff.

The thought of the shipping line's staff brought to his mind Trehane's comment that the secretary was a "high official, too important to handle details." But he had not been too important to write the biography, although, since it was as characterless as if it had come from *Who's Who*, the imputation was that he barely knew Ulmann. Why, if he was so important, did he write the biography himself? And he was not too important to dictate the letter to Swendstrom, and deal with the details. And quickly, too.

"Quickly" served as a reminder that, no matter how long-range this affair had been, Medford must deal as Trehane would deal; he must not forget immediate time elements, must not repeat his reprehensible lapse in not having read the Thames' body autopsy report. Beneath his question to the captain he began a rough of a cable to Trehane:

AT WHAT HOUR . . .

Medford's hand came abruptly away from the paper, away from the cable that would never be sent, and went into his pocket. He withdrew the envelope he had taken from the doctor's cabin and stared at it.

Then he went across the room and pushed a bell.

Heinz showed up, not quickly.

Medford said, "I should like to see the elderly stewardess who also serves as a practical nurse."

"Ah?" The steward looked sleepy, and stubborn. "What is her name, sir?"

"I suggest you ask the captain. He knows who is a practical nurse among the stewards and stewardesses, even if they don't know themselves."

"Ah." Heinz looked briefly bright, but then he dimmed again. "Frau Schmidt. She is undoubtedly sleeping. It is the rest hour. For everyone," he added, making the matter clear.

"Please wake her," Medford said. "Instantly. And bring her here."

"Yes, sir." Apparently the direct line was necessary.

Heinz reappeared, no more than five minutes later, with a puffing Frau Schmidt in tow. "Yes, sir?" she said.

Medford said, "Thank you, Heinz," waited to see the last of the steward's back, and then said, "Sit down, Frau Schmidt."

"Thank you. Those stairs . . ." She plumped her heavy bottom into a chair.

"How is Dr. Swendstrom?"

"Recovering. Very much better."

"Good. Do you think I might talk with him?"

"You might ask the doctor. Dr. Ow-ings." She looked dubious. "But even if it didn't harm him, sir, I don't think it would be any good. For you, I mean. He's only conscious for brief moments, and very—cloudy, you say?"

"Yes. I see. Well, then, going back to Dr. Ulmann. What time did he die?"

"I told you, sir. A little after seven in the evening."

"On Saturday?"

"On Saturday the twelfth."

"I see. Is there any way to prove that?"

"Prove . . ." She stared at him. "Well, I sent for the captain, and he was there when I took the doctor's pulse and tried to get a sign of breath on a mirror. I'm sure he—"

"I'm sure," Medford said, and left before she had heaved herself out of the deep chair.

The captain was no longer either vehement or pleading. He examined Medford with recaptured frigidity, and said, "Again?"

"Sorry to interrupt," Medford said, "but some questions—"

"It is more than an interruption; it is a disturbance." His frown deepened, apparently as a result of his English, and then the imposition of being forced to the hated language

157

caused him added frigid irritation. "This," he said, "is the rest period." He was fully dressed and sitting at his desk.

"Sorry. This is important. I have some ques—"

"This, Mr. Medford, is the rest period." He picked up his cigar, and bent over his papers.

"And if your ship was sinking, would you rest, sir?"

The narrow head came up; the ascetic face bore a small cold smile. "Are we sinking, Mr. Medford? At anchor in the Genua harbor?"

"I used an analogy. In my profession, as in yours, there are times during which we do not rest. Murder is one of those times."

"Swendstrom is dead?"

"Swendstrom is recovering. Ulmann was murdered."

"Really?" The smile didn't waver. "I doubt it. Have you proof?"

"That's why I've come to you."

"To me?" The smile left, and with it went his color.

"Yes, with a few questions. At what time, please, did Dr. Ulmann die?"

"In the evening. The night before we reached Southampton, which puts it at Saturday."

"The exact time, please."

"I don't know. I am not a doctor. Unlike everyone else aboard who if they're doctors seem to consider themselves lawyers, and if they're detectives seem to consider—"

"As nearly as possible, taking into account that you are not a doctor."

"A little after seven o'clock."

"Have you any proof of that?"

The captain stared up at him. "I am the master. My word on this ship—"

"Proof in a court of law."

"My word—" He considered and then said, "The time of death is noted in the log. Naturally. And logs do not lie."

"And what is the time in the log?"

The captain closed his eyes, and with the disappearance of those bits of blue ice, what remained was totally white. Then he opened them and quoted, " 'Twelve minutes past nineteen hundred, on Saturday, January twelfth, in the presence of one stewardess, Frau Elsie Schmidt, and the master of the M. S. *Tilburg*.' "

And why hadn't he said that in the first place? Medford considered the erectly seated figure, and said, "Thank you. And when did you report the death to your home office?"

"Immediately." The captain eyed Medford's brows, which remained suspended, and added stiffly, "In the log the cable is noted as having been dispatched at nineteen fifty-three o'clock."

"I see. Now—" Medford paused. He was attaching undue importance to his next question, he felt, but he couldn't help himself. A negative answer wouldn't destroy his theory, but a positive one would greatly strengthen it. He said, "Have you ever before had a death, reportedly from 'food poisoning,' aboard the *Tilburg?*"

Medford knew before the captain answered that he had not been taken by surprise. He had expected and feared the question, and all his reserve did nothing to hide the fact. He said, with an air of numbness, "A little over two years ago a steward named Willy Schoeck died aboard. Dr. Ulmann diagnosed food poisoning."

"Um? And have you reported this—coincidence—to your home office?" He realized instantly that the question was foolish, and its foolishness restored the captain's poise.

"Reported?" the captain asked icily. "It was reported at the time, *naturally*, and I see no reason to report what you call 'coincidences' to my principals, who can presumably read, remember, and judge."

"Quite," Medford said. "One more thing"—he ignored the captain's weary sigh—"have there been any changes in personnel in the last week? Outside of Dr. Swendstrom, of course?"

"No."

"Thank you again." As he closed the door behind him, Medford noted that the captain was still staring at him, looking far less assured.

4

"I got married," Elizabeth Smith said.

The third personality had held. She was contained, quiet, grown-up. The smart-aleck and the shy child had both disappeared. But she looked unhappy. "I got married," she repeated.

"Yes?"

She stared at Max, but she wasn't seeing him. "I thought I was dreaming it last night, but I know now that it is the truth. It happened."

" 'Truth,' " Max quoted, " 'is that which exists.' So you got married?"

"Right after my grandfather died. It seemed wrong to me at the time, I think. It still does. But it shouldn't, should it? Marriage isn't wrong?"

"It depends. On whom one marries and other things. It might have seemed wrong to you because of predicate thinking. Forgive the jargon. What I mean is that if your grandfather had impressed upon you that any association with a man was wrong, you might have felt that even marriage was wrong. Or there might have been another reason."

"Well"—a composed, entirely adult smile came coolly to her small face—"I had over twenty-five thousand dollars from my grandfather."

"And you thought you were being married for it?"

"I don't know if I thought it then, but I did later. When I married I thought I was the luckiest person in the world.

I had been—I'm sure of this—plain, drab, a totally uninteresting child, and feeling myself loved by someone fascinating and sought-after, I became quite pretty. Still rather childish, but really very pretty. I think my husband was surprised, and even gratified."

"And who was your husband?"

"That part gets left out of the dream. I remember his outline and a hundred facts and impressions but not his face. In the dream, he actually had a blank where a face is."

"Hypnosis would bring it back, but it will come without that. You are very likely to see the face itself in another dream. And soon. The resistance becomes less strong during sleep, so people recall things in dreams that they forget when awake."

"Resistance? But why should I resist?"

"Pain," he said promptly. "The memory is painful and you are repressing it."

"But I'm not. I'm trying desperately to remember."

"I'd much rather not get into psychological phraseology. Put it this way: In certain sorts of physical injury, like the rupture of a spinal disc, for instance, people experience muscle contractions. The nerve, painfully pinched by the out-of-place disc, causes the muscle to move away, so easing the pain. That is analogous. Or take the known cases of people who have been quite blind only because they did not want to see. Nothing wrong with their visual mechanisms. Seeing was simply too painful for them. Another analogy. In your case, your inner mind is trying to spare your outer mind a memory of pain."

The small face was unhappy. "So I'm a neurotic?"

"Not necessarily. Probably not at all. Neurotic anxiety exists, of course, and then people become afraid of something that does not exist; they build up bogies. But there is such a thing as objective anxiety, in which people are afraid of very real things. Their fear may lead them to repression, and the dreadful extent of the reality may be such that repression is the mind's only way out. . . . You don't remember his face. His name?"

She shook her head, her face remote.

"Things about him?"

"Oh, yes. Very definitely. He was English. He had left England because he had to, but if I found out why, I don't remember that. He spent my money . . ."

In her pause, Max thought that, as always with poor little Beth Smith, the story was usual, mundane—which, of course, didn't make it any easier for the victim.

"But there was one thing good—or maybe I mean honest —about him. He loved me. That is, he came to love me. Or maybe he just came to think of me as a somewhat valuable possession, even after the money was gone. Because he fought the divorce, and I think it really mattered to him."

"Divorce?" Max wasn't sure why he was surprised. She didn't seem to have had sufficient gumption to move out of such a situation. But the ability to make the decision was probably a foreshadowing of the present personality.

"Oh, yes, I divorced him. And, as I say, it wounded him. I think he felt he had created me—like Pygmalion, you know?—and that I belonged to him. And so he loved me, if that is love."

"It is a twisted form of love."

"And despite my unusual strength, my ability to divorce him over his objections, I became weak again. He promised me money if I'd go to England—"

She stopped abruptly, surprise plain on her face—"If I *came* to England. So I *do* know England, I suppose. But I don't remember it."

"It'll come."

"I suppose so. Well, he must have gone back to England, but I don't seem to remember. And yet I know that I came to England because he promised to return some of my money if I came. I don't think I believed he would give any of it back, and yet—I came. And then, when I got there, and he didn't give me money, I behaved as if I *had* expected money, and I got upset, and—sick." Her eyes lifted to his. "Neurotic," she said.

"Not necessarily." He spoke earnestly, experiencing the

pain that his patients' pain often brought him. This too great sympathy, this inability to achieve the necessary detachment, caused him a good deal of worry. He wanted, above anything on earth, to be a doctor. He wanted to be a good doctor. But, although he cared little about the rest of the world, his patients became deeply important to him, almost an extension of himself, and he feared that the lack of divorcement might make him less capable.

"Well, he sent me to a psychoanalyst."

"Which doesn't necessarily mean you needed one. And if you did, that still doesn't mean—"

"I needed him." She gave a decisive little nod.

"But association with this ex-husband could have so overwhelmed you, so increased your anxiety that it reached the traumatic stage. And still it needn't have been a phobia —irrational, that is."

"The psychoanalyst was kind. A very kind man. To me and to . . ." A look of puzzlement came over her face, and then, right before Max's eyes, she performed the outward mechanisms of repression: Her lips set, her body tensed, her hands clasped and tightened. Her body became angular and tightly unrelaxed and her face turned wooden. Through newly thin lips, barely parted, she said, "My husband's name was Robert."

5

Medford's splendidly uniformed messenger took longer than usual to arrive but he finally came and then went off with the two cables, one of them Medford's new version to Trehane:

ADVISE GERMANS TO EFFECT IMMEDIATE ARREST KURT
VON WINCKEL SECRETARY OF SHIPPING LINE FOR COM-
PLICITY IN MURDER OF ULMANN STOP VON WINCKELS
LETTER TO SWENDSTROM PARENTHESIS IN POSSESSION
OF SHIPS MEDICAL OFFICER PARENTHESIS IS POST-
MARKED FORTY ONE MINUTES BEFORE DEATH OF UL-
MANN STOP LETTER REFERS PREMATURELY TO FACT OF
ULMANNS DEATH WILL TELEPHONE YOU AT SIX THIS
EVENING GENOA TIME

Then he went in search of tea.

Tea, his little guidebook had told him, was served on the
Enclosed Promenade Aisle, Portside. But one look at that
alleyway's dreary coldness prepared him for its desertion.
Through the windows on his left he saw the assemblage,
and entered the Veranda Café. The Veranda Café, over-
looking the empty swimming pool and the deserted "Lido"
Deck, was warmer and slightly more cheerful.

Medford spotted Max Owings in the center of the room,
sitting at a large table with a number of people. He looked
unhappy, but brightened at the sight of Medford and called
out, "Over here. Come and join us."

Medford ambled over, nodded at Mr. Pitkethly, a Malayan gentleman, a Chinese lady, a pretty half-breed girl,
an Italian woman in severe black, a very dignified and
handsome Englishman in his sixties, three English matrons,
and a lady who looked like a horse and smelled like a
dynamited perfume factory. Max performed introductions,
most of which Medford didn't catch—largely, he suspected,
because Owings, with little idea of the names, was performing a slight-of-tongue trick. But the Chinese lady was
named Madame Hausman, which tied up with the captain's
biography. Medford was interrupted in his attempt to tie
that irrelevancy into opium, sick and dead doctors, amnesia,
and conked ladies by the arrival of Heinz. Medford ordered
tea, and sat down.

"Tea," Owings said sadly. "Hate it." He nodded at his

164

glass. "Beer. Don't like that either, but it seems too early for a highball."

"Not a bit of it," said the English gentleman. He was sipping from a tall glass of very dark liquid. A triple Scotch, Medford decided, and noting the network of fine red veins on his face also decided that the drink was one in a life-time's long series. The Englishman said, "This is the sort of day that requires desperate measures just to stay normally healthy."

Pitkethly also had a highball. He said, "I agree. This is making me feel extremely healthy, thank you." So presumably the Englishman had stood him to it. His speech was slightly thick, and something about his red-faced "healthiness" caused Medford to feel a distaste that went beyond any reaction to drunkenness. The Scotsman, he thought, was losing his inhibitions and might soon be a very nasty character.

Owings said, "Mr. Clarkson is sitting with Miss Elkin." He looked forlorn.

Medford decided that Owings had felt unnecessary in their company, had been routed. He said, "How is Miss Elkin?"

"Fine. All better. I prescribed dinner in the dining room. And we are to have dancing and festivity this evening."

"Why?"

"I can't imagine." Owings looked guardedly at Madame Hausman.

Mr. Pitkethly felt no such instinct of tact. He said, with something resembling a giggle, "Presumably the captain feels the need of exercise."

The Englishman said, "Haw."

Madame Hausman's mask did not crack. She said, "I think it is so good for one to dress. Especially on a dreary day. Clothes *brighten* things."

The Italian lady said dubiously, "You sink so?" Medford noticed that her only ornament was a small gold cross worn on a chain around her neck.

Max Owings said to the Italian lady, "Yes, signorina.

There is medical truth in that." The Italian woman looked warmed, although Medford felt sure that her style of dress would not change. Max turned to Medford: "Dressing up is what I prescribed for Miss Elkin."

The horselike young woman said, "I quite agree. Also." Medford felt that if "dressing up" meant, as it usually did to ladies, "dressing down," the horsefaced one would have to attend the evening's festivities in the nude. At the moment the over-the-table view of her showed only a wine-red affair that worked like two slings, and the prominent dot on each high pocket suggested that that was all she wore.

One of the English ladies was knitting. She was several stone heavier than the horse, and the visible upper half of her was clearly boned and perhaps even otherwise supported. She addressed her knitting: "I'm *sure* you agree, Fräulein Gotthelf. Do tell us what you have in store for us this evening."

Medford examined the crimps in the English lady's hair, and decided that, crimps or not, she was probably very pleasant.

Madame Hausman said, "Oh, no! We must all surprise one another."

Pitkethly looked vulgar, the Englishman looked absent, the pretty Malayan girl looked amused.

Owings looked fed up. He watched Medford finish his tea, gave his half-full glass a little push, and said eagerly, "Finished? A walk around the deck?"

Medford would have liked more tea. He said, "Quite."

They strolled around the boat deck. Medford said, "Until we freeze. . . . I'm glad the nice Miss Elkin has recovered. The stewardess tells me that Swendstrom is coming along nicely too."

"Very well, yes."

"Can I question him?"

"Oh, no. He's not in *that* good order. He has only the briefest of conscious periods, and then he's foggy. But possibly tomorrow morning. A good night's sleep . . ."

"And Miss Smith?"

Owings' mouth tightened. "She was doing fine, and then . . ." He shook his head.

"Tell me about it."

"Well . . ." and with his usual reportorial ability he gave Medford an almost word-for-word reprise of his afternoon's interview with Elizabeth Smith. He ended: "Her husband's name was Robert, she said. Then, without warning, she set up a barrier, instituted repression proper."

Medford said, "Um. And when may I talk to her?"

"For the moment, I fear the results. Wait a while, will you? It'll all come back, you know. She can't hold it at bay much longer. Perhaps"—he looked dubious—"it is better to have it come naturally. Some little event, word, association, is bound to release the trigger soon. Incidentally, I advised her also to come to dinner tonight. She too needs the gaiety of pretty clothes and music, even if it is all schmaltzy-waltzy. And the repressed state will be very temporary, I think. A few hours' set back, that's all."

Medford noted the tenderness in his voice. He would have thought Dr. Owings had a special feeling for Miss Smith if he hadn't heard the warmth on other occasions. And yet . . . He said conversationally, "She's a pretty girl, isn't she?"

"No," Owings said, almost with annoyance, "she's a handsome young woman who deserves care and attention."

"Oh, quite," Medford said, in surprise. "Quite. Well, Doctor, if you'll excuse me, I have an errand ashore."

6

Medford collected a landing card from the blond young man in the purser's enclosure, and made the damp trip ashore. He found a cab and was conveyed through a hole in the forbidding wall and along the *corso* until the driver stopped in front of a petrol station. There, he indicated, Medford would find a public phone.

Medford waited in the cold darkness until the driver had driven off. He felt the precaution was fairly idiotic, but someone aboard the *Tilburg* was a murderer, and one took idiotic precautions when trying to capture murderers.

The call went through with a maximum of Italian imprecations, and a good deal of polite English delay. Medford finally said, "Trehane?"

"Here, old boy. Hell of a mess, isn't it? Opium, indeed." He took a clearly audible breath and said, "Have duly advised the German police in Hamburg to arrest Herr Von Winckel. Hope you're right."

Now, what could one say to that? "Quite," Medford said. "Seems evident, you know."

"But unchecked," said the checking one. "Ah, well. What's next?"

"Report to the super. As follows, please: Ulmann was murdered. Murderer is still aboard, or so chances indicate since there have been no changes in personnel. It seems clear that Kurt Von Winckel ordered Ulmann killed, but the actual murderer either procrastinated, or was in some way delayed. And Von Winckel either assumed his instructions had been obeyed, or got some sort of misleading message to that effect. At any rate, he wanted one particular man to replace Ulmann—it's worth considering the possibility that the murder took place simply *because* Von Winckel—or Von Winckel and his superiors—wanted a particular man in that position. At any rate, Von Winckel couldn't wait for confirmation because the ship, although held over for one day, would still not be in England long enough to permit of delay. So he wrote to Swendstrom confirming that, according to their exchange of telegrams, Swendstrom was to replace the 'dead' Ulmann, who was merely moribund at that moment. Actual cable notifying of Ulmann's death was dispatched at seven minutes before eight o'clock that night. Please note, Trehane, that not only was his letter postmarked before the death of Ulmann had been reported to him, but there had been an exchange of cables even before that."

"That does seem confirmation, doesn't it?" Trehane cheered up even further: "And we ought to be able to check those cables."

"Oh, quite. Now, it would seem that Von Winckel, no matter how close his time schedule, was taking an incomprehensible chance in sending that cable and writing that letter, but I think that may be accounted for by the fact that he possibly had precedent for feeling safe. Some two and a half years ago a steward, name of Willy Schoeck"—he spelled it—"also died of what Ulmann diagnosed as 'food poisoning.' I certainly don't know the statistics on the frequency of death from poisoned food, but I should think it's not a very high figure, and happening on this boat makes it seem rather an unlikely coincidence—"

"Oh, rather!" Trehane said. His voice was brightening by the minute.

"—so it's possible that it was nothing of the sort, that Von Winckel had a hand in what was really the murder of the steward, that it was not investigated, and that he thought Ulmann's death would be similarly ignored."

"I'll check," Trehane said happily.

"Do. A further possibility arises—that Ulmann himself was implicated, since he declared the previous death accidental."

169

"Oh." Trehane retreated to dubiousness. "But that's rather assuming, isn't it?"

"If one doesn't make assumptions," Medford said, his voice gentle, "one would have nothing to check, would one?"

"Huh?"

"Never mind. What about my questions in the cable of last night?"

"My God, Medford, I've only had it a few hours—"

"All right, all right."

"—but the question about time of Swendstrom's death is easy enough, of course. Had you forgotten?"

Medford counted to five. Then he said, "I never read the autopsy report."

"You never *read*—"

"No, Trehane. When did he die?"

"I must say . . ."

"Well, say it, please, and then tell me *when*."

"They refused to pin it down but put it probably at Saturday, the twelfth. 'Probably between eight in the morning and midnight of that day.'—I can't think how it happened that you didn't read it. Well, I also have the answer to another of your questions: Elizabeth Smith's ticket was purchased at the Bond Street office late on Saturday, the twelfth. No one can remember who did the purchasing, probably because it *was* late, and they were concentrating on their week ends."

"Ah. Well, thank you, Trehane."

"But I don't see what good that information does you?"

"I think it helps. But . . ." There was a little silence while Medford put things together.

His assumptions that Swendstrom's murderer had assumed his identity—that he was the ship's Swendstrom—was strengthened. If the Latinish young man had killed him, he had time to take the real Swendstrom's papers, collect his Southampton ticket, and board. Also, by being booked so late, E. Smith was more possibly a tie-in. That was too haphazard to report to Trehane, however. "I think those answers help," he said. "And the question about Gonzales?"

"My God, Medford, I've only had the cable—"

"All right, all right. Well, you can tell the super that, although I have very little concrete beyond the implication of Von Winckel, I have hope of tying the matter up at this end."

"You mean you have definite suspects? But if you have nothing concrete—"

"Just tell him that, Trehane." Medford's voice remained gentle. "Oddly enough, he'll understand. Good-bye, Trehane. Happy dreams."

But for all his querulous bickering, for all his unnecessary checking, Trehane was a good and helpful worker. At nine-thirty that evening Medford received a cable:

ROBERTO GONZALES EMIGRATED TO CANADA THEN SEEMS TO HAVE ENTERED STATES ILLEGALLY PRACTICED MEDICINE IN DETROIT WITHOUT LICENSE OF COURSE STOP WAS IMPLICATED IN NEW ABORTION AFFAIR SKIPPED OUT SUCCESSFULLY STOP EVENTUALLY TRACED BY DETROIT POLICE TO LOS ANGELES STOP NOT BRILLIANT POLICE WORK SINCE HE WAS ACTING IN CINEMA ALIAS ROBERT RAMON BUT PRESUMABLY WITH HIS OWN FACE STOP AGAIN SKIPPED THIS TIME TRACE LOST STOP EX WIFE INSISTED HE RETURNED HERE BUT ASSERTION DOUBTED SINCE HAVING NO VISA HE COULD NOT HAVE GOT EXIT PERMIT STOP TRAIL ENDS THERE

TREHANE

Oh, no, it doesn't, Medford thought. The trail ended *here*, on the M. S. *Tilburg*. It fitted:

The poisoned gentleman below decks was Roberto Gonzales, alias Robert Ramon, alias Nils Swendstrom. Elizabeth Smith was very possibly his ex-wife. Her ticket had been bought after the murder of the real Swendstrom, when Gonzales had decided to assume Swendstrom's identity. So her ex-husband wanted to take her along—because he loved her? Because she was a danger if left in England?

Possibly for both reasons? Whichever or both she could very well be his ex-wife. ("My husband's name was Robert." And "I am a Californian.") Her husband had sent her to a doctor, very likely to Dr. Barkland, whom he knew since the Terrence Clinic affair. (The similar name, "Clarkson," had penetrated her mental lapse far enough to frighten her.) Then Gonzales had killed Barkland. Did she know he was dead? Did she know Gonzales had killed him? Had she actually witnessed it? Well, although on the one hand Gonzales took some care of her (he had loved her, she told Owings, or at least had thought of her as a valuable possession even after he ran through her money), he probably had pushed her down the stairs, and that might have been to put her out of the running, so she couldn't report a murder.

And therefore—now what?

Medford considered the problem. Arrest Gonzales immediately? Could he prove murder? If not, on what charge? Impersonation? No. Material witness? But the man was not movable, not even questionable until morning, according to Owings. When questioned he might throw light on the still unclear murder of Ulmann, the probable murder of Willy Schoek, the smuggling of opium. On the other hand, if Medford put him under arrest, or advertised that he intended to do so, other person or persons implicated in the murder of Ulmann and in the transportation of opium might be frightened off.

Medford decided on patience until the morning.

```
GENUA       20TH JANUARY
A Gala will be held this evening
in the Lounge.  The captain
respectfully commands that guests
wear evening dress.  Festivities
will commence at ten-thirty.  May
a good time be enjoyed by all!
```

May it, indeed! Medford thought, recalling the bulletin-board notice. He suspected that the Gala hadn't really "commenced" quite yet although—he peeked at his watch —it was after eleven. (Which brought it perilously near Monday, the *Tilburg*'s scheduled day of departure and Medford's personal Day of Decision. Break this thing open by midday or chance traveling to the mouth of the Suez Canal to Port Saïd, once called the Wickedest City in the East, and now probably the dirtiest and undoubtedly the dullest.)

Although it hadn't really got off the ground, the Gala struck Medford as being astounding, in toto and in its parts. His first touch of astonishment had come with the announcement itself, when he discovered, in the German version of the "respectful command," that the word for evening dress was *Gesellschaftsanzug*. However promising, that had been the merest beginning.

The captain had not yet danced, although Owings' promised "schmaltzy-waltzy" music was flowing oilily over the lounge. The captain's dance routines, Medford supposed, remembering Owings' expression as he reported the captain's gyrations, would probably cap the evening.

But it needed no capping.

In considering its parts, his astonishment sprang from a number of items, which he had not sorted into the order of crescendo: The captain's air of gleaming joviality was enough to confound one. Then there was the women's appearance. The German horse-lady had done the impossible by contriving, after all, to lessen her bodice. She now wore the same type of double-sling affair (Miss Smith had advised him, her face admirably composed, that it was called a halter, and the word's terrible appropriateness had reduced Max Owings and Mr. Clarkson to schoolboyish guffaws), but the current version was composed of two patches of black satin that made no attempt to cover her; where it crossed at her breasts and joined the short, horribly tight skirt, it left large gaps through which the skin of her waist and ribs showed. ("A midriff halter," Elizabeth Smith added demurely.) The horsy lady danced constantly with the chief engineer, a stocky gentleman somewhat shorter than she, and despite his staid and dated fox trot (which he used impartially for schottische, scherzo, and polka, all that had been so far offered) she contrived an astounding amount of motion. The reflections off the black satin were blinding.

Madame Hausman was blinding in a more agreeable way. Her dress, high-necked and tight in Chinese fashion, was cloth of gold. Medford, knowing nothing whatever about the matter, suspected nevertheless that it was frighteningly expensive. Her stockings appeared to have been woven of spun silver and her shoes matched. She wore gold clips in her high hairdress and long diamond earrings. They alone, thought Medford (who *did* know something about that matter), would have caused him enough surprise for one evening.

But Miss Smith, the Italian lady, two matrons, and Miss Elkin had supplied more. Both Miss Smith and Miss Elkin turned out to be attractive—Miss Elkin mostly because of her figure, which was, as one of the English matrons had said, "divine," and Miss Smith because she was beautiful. She wore black velvet, tight to the waist and then very full. The dress might have seemed too young for her but the arm sling she had devised was of brilliant red silk, and it made the outfit more suitable to her type. Above the simple curved neckline, her face was the color of pearls, made even more arresting by her beautiful black eyes, and surmounted, over a high and serene forehead, by a simply swept back mass of very dark hair.—If nothing else had amazed him, his own mental description of Miss Smith would have done it.

Two of the matrons wore dresses so short, so fancy, and so tight as to cause him speculation as to how they had got in and, even more, as to how, short of scissors, they would get out. And the Italian lady, who had appeared only briefly, had nevertheless contributed her own touch. To the black dress, which, as he had been sure, had not changed, she too had added red. Her scarf was a darker color than Miss Smith's, and the effect had fallen far short of Miss Smith's, but he decided that the attempt was probably unusual, and he felt warm toward Owings for having brought it about.

Mr. Pitkethly had supplied his touch by getting unbelievably drunk at a very early hour, and disappearing with a gait that made Medford feel seasick.

The arthritic English gentleman of the great dignity wore a belaced and beruffled shirt beneath his evening jacket. It seemed to require no tie. The English lady with the massive bosom who had been knitting at teatime was now sitting at their table of seven, and, following Medford's glance, advised him, with an air of sympathy, that the shirt was from the Philippines where similar ones were always worn in the evenings.

"Ah," said Medford. "And what is *that?*"

"That" was the outfit of a dark-complexioned gentleman across the room. It was comprised of blue silk trousers, a magnificent overblouse of blue woven with silver, and a silver hat that looked vaguely Jewish.

"A baju," his guide murmured, looking as if she wished she had something to knit. She brought her glance up from her hands and added, "Malayan evening dress. We were stationed there for three years, y'know. Bajus can be quite magnificent."

"So I see."

"That one is a mere beginning," she assured him. "The name has always puzzled me, though. It was once applied to a tribe of Malayans who were really notorious pirates. Not to worry, however."

"Oh, no," Medford agreed nonsensically, "not at all. But if we must have native costume I prefer *that.*"

The English lady glanced at the part Malayan, part Filipino young woman. She had chosen to wear something that was probably Filipino, all ruffles and colorful embroidery. The effect was—

"Charming," the English lady and Mr. Clarkson murmured in the same breath.

"I," Medford said, "am not in native costume"—he

indicated his blue suit—"because I was not properly equipped. The captain has forgiven me, however."

Miss Elkin and Miss Smith said together and with the same inflection, "But you look *very* nice."

Clarkson laughed. He was handsomely pink above an ancient, very nearly green dinner jacket. He said, "At least we are all most *simpatico*, to employ native terms. We seem to be on the same wave length."

Unconsciously all the six who were on that wave length glanced at the seventh, who was most certainly not. The purser was still yellow, and mentally far away. Unlike the others, who had brandies, he was drinking coffee, and in quantity.

"What's *that?*" Medford asked.

"What?" Owings looked around to find Medford's newest discovery.

"No, the noise," the English lady said. She too was listening.

"The dreadful music," Owings suggested.

"The high sound. *Above* the music," the English lady explained.

"A dreadful violin?" Elizabeth Smith asked.

"No." Miss Elkin looked alert. Medford thought that her little ears were actually pointing.

"It sounds like a Brunei woman in labor," Mr. Clarkson said. Then he looked understandably confounded. "How idiotic of me!" Without a breath's pause he added, "Don't look, my dear. Don't look!"

But he was too late: Miss Elkin was looking. She said, "It's—good heaven! Oh, good heaven!"

Medford and Owings both stood up. They were the first to react physically to the new entry in fancy dress.

Mrs. Pitkethly wore, Max realized, a nightgown. It was white cotton, much too big for her. Her hair was in pigtails. The sound was issuing from her. It was high, and it might have been called a scream but it sounded more like keening.

176

Beth Smith said, "She's bleeding. My God. She's bleeding. My God."

The Englishwoman said, "Doctor . . ."

Sure, I'm a doctor, Max thought, but where's the blood coming from? He remained glued behind the table for at least another ten seconds. He was (insanely, insanely, he told himself) inspecting the apparition.

The mouth in the little monkey's face was held very wide, and out of it came the high sound. But the mouth was crooked. Her jaw is broken, Max decided. Her jaw is broken, but where does that blood on the gown and on the floor come from? Surely not the jaw. As he finally started forward (had the Englishwoman pushed him? he wondered much later), he saw: one of the long pigtails had been yanked almost free of the head. The blood came from there.

Mrs. Pitkethly achieved the center of the empty floor, and crumpled there, a small but billowing bag of bloody laundry. As Owings reached her and knelt, Medford behind him said, "Your patient . . ."

Owings glanced up impatiently. He said, "I know . . ." but his voice faded as he saw what Medford meant.

The ship's substitute doctor was standing in the doorway, and he was no longer quite so handsome. He stood there, a bewildered-looking man in wrinkled candy-cane-striped pajamas much too small for him. He had a two-day growth of beard, bloodshot eyes, hairy ankles and shin-bones, and the hair on his head no longer flowed smoothly back from a perfect widow's peak. He said, "Someone's killing someone on my ceiling. It hurts my head. Someone's screaming on my head."

"Oh, God," Owings said. "Get him back to bed, can you, Medford?"

"Robert. Robert!"

Medford swung around. Beth Smith, standing very straight, her face as white as that of the man called Swendstrom, was staring at his pajama-clad figure. Her eyes, much too widely held, swung down to Owings. "Doctor," she said, "he's Robert."

"Robert *Ramon*," Miss Elkin said, with an insane air of instruction, "Robert Ramon, the movie actor!"

"And he hit you, there at the pool?" Medford asked.

"I smelled cologne," she said. "But that isn't really enough for an accusation, is it?"

"But he may have been trying to kill you. Because you had recognized—"

Ramon-Swendstrom-Gonzales said, in a dull tone, "It's he who tried to kill." He pointed at the purser. "He tried to kill me."

The captain stepped onto the dance floor, but not in the way Medford had imagined it would be. Joviality gone, his customary authority had replaced it. "This is quite enough," he said. "This is a most—most unseemly—"

The purser had opened and closed his mouth several times. He now achieved sound, although it was not very reminiscent of human speech. He squeaked, "He lies! He lies! He—"

The captain stared coldly down at the purser. "Probably he tells the truth. You have always been mixed up in something. You have always been in the center of the something disreputable that goes on aboard my ship. Drugs, probably. That you tried to kill does not surprise me, not in—"

The purser, apparently incapable of standing, managed to fling his hand up and point a quivering finger at the captain. "*You* speak!" he squealed. "You murderer, *you* accuse?"

The captain opened a white mouth in a white face and said, "*Halten Sie ihre Schnauze!*"

"You killed Hausman!"

"It was an accident!" His first self-defense in five years opened a floodgate. The white mouth stretched thin and wide, and through it he yelled, "Accident, accident, accident! I didn't even send him, he insisted upon going! *You* know that"—he looked around the room and said, "Ulmann's gone. Hausman's gone. They're all gone. You"—

he focused on the chief engineer, who had apparently been frozen into position, unfortunately with his arm around the bare waist of Fräulein Gotthelf. "You, Lorenz, you tell them!"

The chief engineer seemed to come awake. He removed his arm, shook his head, turned and walked to a corner, and sat down.

"You don't understand!" the captain yelled. "No one has understood!"

"No one has understood." The purser nodded his head. "How many masters can I serve? You?" Astonishingly, he spat on the floor. "Not *you!* But you're the master. Von Winckel? But he doesn't understand how difficult it all is. And him"—the quivering finger came up and stabbed wildly in Gonzales' direction—"he *pretends* not to understand. What was I to do?"

At Owings' knee, Mrs. Pitkethly regained consciousness, moaned, and said, "He tried to kill me."

"No doubt," Owings said grimly. "Medford, shouldn't someone restrain Pitkethly before he does more harm?"

"Yes," Medford said. Where to start?

Beth Smith said, in a whispering echo, "Did Robert try to kill me?"

Gonzales shook his head. The motion cost him obvious effort. His voice also was a whisper. "No," he said sibilantly. "But afterward . . . I just had to keep you quiet, you see? You do see?"

Medford said to the room at large, "We'll have a little order." He turned on Gonzales. "You killed Dr. Clarence Barkland? And Nils Swendstrom?"

Gonzales looked at him blankly.

"Dr. Barkland? Dr. Barkland is dead?" Beth Smith sat down as if she were very old. "But he couldn't have killed Dr. Barkland. He was a good man, a dear, good man, and kind to me and to Robert, too. Robert got jealous of him, but he couldn't, he couldn't—"

"He was trying to prove to you that you didn't need me!" Gonzales' whisper was fierce, and Medford thought that Gonzales might be presenting a refreshingly different motive for murder.

Miss Smith said tonelessly, "He said we had to get away for a while. He said Dr. Barkland approved. And he hurried me onto the boat, and didn't explain much. I wasn't even supposed to know him, and I was so confused. And then on the little boat—"

The tender, Medford thought.

"—I insisted on talking to him, and it made him angry. And when he's angry . . . Did you push me down the stairs, Robert?"

"He did, he did!" The purser's squeal was vicious. "I saw it!"

"Did you indeed?" Medford inquired. "But you kept that little secret?"

The purser closed his trembling mouth.

Gonzales looked down at the purser with something resembling contempt. He said, "He's just a liar. He wanted something from me, but he was so scared he couldn't even tell me what." He reeled, put a hand out into space, and somehow regained his balance.

Owings said, "For God's sake, Medford, get that man back to bed. Somebody take Miss Smith to her cabin. And Miss Elkin has fainted, Clarkson. You"—he addressed the young chief mate—"will you help me get this woman to a cabin? Not," he added grimly, "her own cabin."

MONDAY

Medford nodded at the bulletin board and said to the blond young purser's assistant, "And who posted that bit of nonsense?"

"Bitte?"

Max materialized at Medford's side. He said, "That boy knows the phrase book, but he never learned the appropriate places for his assortment."

The assistant purser said to Max, *"Bitte, machen Sie sich verständlich."*

"What did he say?"

Max sighed. "He wants your immortal words translated. Oh, well." He stumbled into German, flinched at the young man's instant flow, and finally said to Medford, "All I get is that the captain's word is law."

"He couldn't possibly have put it more incorrectly. This"—Medford indicated his splendidly uniformed messenger boy—*"this* is the word of the law."

The Italian cop, come into his own, beamed resplendently.

The German youth looked dumfounded.

It took several minutes and three languages, but Medford finally got across his points: 1. The *Tilburg* was going nowhere whatever; 2. The captain's word, at least for the moment, had no more weight than a mutineer's; 3. The notice was to come down.

The assistant purser removed the notice. His smooth, extremely German face registered mutinous disapproval at such an unclear chain of command. Medford was reminded of the boy's immediate superior, who had, a very short time before, filled Medford's ears with plaintive whines about *his* unclear chain of command.

Owings said, "How is your 'confusion worse confounded?' "

" 'Confusion unconfus'd,' " Medford said. "Yours was Milton and I have no idea whose mine was."

"Well, it approaches the finality of facthood. As that arthritic toffeenose said to me a few minutes ago, 'One always puts these confounded blokes in their places eventually.' I think he meant that crime doesn't pay."

" 'Toffeenose'?"

"Stuffed shirt. Have you never met an Englishman, never come into contact with vulgar English slang?"

"Not that close into contact. Toffeenose, huh?" He smiled, but he was looking very tired.

Medford examined his tired face and said, "You're a bit off, Dr. Owings? Not feeling tiptop?"

"Weary. I could give you a fistful of quotes. Like, 'Few physicians live well.' Which reminds me—early as it is, I want a drink. Join me?"

Medford hesitated. Then he said, "I'll come along."

Mr. Clarkson had engaged himself in a deck-by-deck search. Consumed by a curiosity for facts, details, fill-ins, explanations, his quarry was Owings or Medford, preferably both. But he missed both men at every turn.

On the boat deck he met Fräulein Gotthelf. She was unusually well covered, and without male companionship, which meant she was alone.

"Good morning," Mr. Clarkson said. When her smile showed no strong yellow teeth and was accompanied by no neigh, he added, "You are feeling well?"

"Yes. Oh, yes. But a little worried. The affair of last night—the affairs, really . . ."

"Yes?"

"Well, my fiancé will be horrified to learn that I was on such a frightful ship."

"Your fiancé?"

"He's so proper, Werner. A man who places much importance on propriety. And that is quite right, don't you think?"

"Quite right," Mr. Clarkson said gravely.

"Werner is engaged in business in Osaka and I am en route there to marry him. He will be *most* disturbed when he learns that I have been exposed to such influences, to such people."

"Indeed. But you yourself have been in no way involved. You must assure him of that."

"Yes." She brightened a little. "Of course, Werner *trusts* me . . ."

"Of *course!*" Mr. Clarkson, feeling himself in danger of explosion, decided that escape was necessary. "You will excuse me?"

He hightailed it for the bar.

Medford and Owings found Mr. Clarkson in the bar. He brightened at the sight of them and said sunnily, "I've been waiting for you two." He looked at the Italian and added dubiously, "Three."

"Feel free to express yourself," Medford told him. "The boss here hasn't a word of English."

Owings said, "What an odd place to expect to find us!"

"Agreed." Mr. Clarkson nodded his pink-and-white head. "Fantastic of me. How are the patients?"

"Miss Elkin," Max said pointedly, "couldn't be better. She merely sustained an understandable shock, which, coming on top of being conked—my pardon, Medford—caused her to relapse slightly." He examined Mr. Clarkson and then relented. He said, with a slight smile, "She also advised me that she is going to lay over in Sarawak for a while."

Mr. Clarkson turned pinker, but rallied quickly. "The use of the phrase 'lay over' seems unfortunate," he said pontifically.

"Don't be a toffeenose." Medford smiled, and Owings jerked a thumb at him and said, "On the other hand, I hear that the law here is taking Miss Smith to England. Don't know why."

"Witness. She is willing," Medford said briefly.

Owings raised his eyebrows. "To what is she a witness?"

"Long story."

"Love to hear it," Mr. Clarkson said promptly. "But first, as a clergyman, may I inquire of Dr. Owings as to the health of the remainder of this hell ship?"

Owings said, "All right, you gossip!" His face relaxed

a little, although it remained noticeably weary. He said to the bartender, "Gin and tonic. Medford?"

"Ginger, please. Too early for me."

"Tomato juice, Mr. Clarkson?"

"Thank you, yes."

"And you, my fine-feathered policeman?" The Italian caught the intonation and perked up. "*Vino?*" he said. The bartender looked disgusted but nodded.

"Now," Owings said, "my dear Mr. Clarkson, you want the gossip?"

Clarkson achieved a high degree of pink-and-white dignity: "I wish only to hear the truth from the mouths of wise men."

"Horses' mouths, huh?"

"I have already had the word from the mouth of the mare.—Never mind, I'll tell you later. So?"

"So," Owings said, "mine is not the secret business of governments, like Medford's, and a report is simple. This hospital ship contains the following: Mrs. Pitkethly, very ill indeed. This afternoon a well-known and highly regarded Italian physician is boarding us. He will probably order her to a local hospital. Poor woman. In addition to a broken jaw—which needs hospital wiring that I cannot manage here—and a badly lacerated scalp, she is a mass of scars, old and new. Also has a rupture. Poor little thing."

"No wonder she was always so frightened," Mr. Clarkson said somberly.

"Yes. And she probably accounted largely for the atmosphere of fear that I felt aboard. Like a miasma."

"If you will forgive me," Medford said, "since after all I wasn't here, I am inclined to think that any atmosphere of fear had a far larger aura than little Mrs. Pitkethly gave out. There were quite a number of people experiencing fear. The purser is an instance."

"Yes," Max said. "Yes, indeed. Well, as for the rest, Miss Elkin is fine; the captain is sick—at heart, I think; and Miss Smith is not well at all. Not well enough to travel, in my opinion."

Medford said, "A formal medical opinion, Doctor?"

"No, damn it. But she needs rest."

"What about the so-called ship's doctor?" Mr. Clarkson asked.

"Held incommunicado," Max said briefly.

"Held—" Mr. Clarkson turned to look at Medford.

"For the moment," Medford said equably. "He's resting."

Max said, "So, Mr. Clarkson, to clear out the ward, the purser has passed beyond my ken, looking very green, and Mr. Pitkethly, even greener, is another who is no longer contained by this ship."

"Mr. Pitkethly," Medford explained, "is in the Genoa jail. He is charged with something that is new to me, but it sounds a bit like 'criminal abuse and mayhem' and I don't think our local friend here likes him."

The uninformed Italian beamed and poured more *vino*.

"Things don't look too good for him," Medford said. "Oh, happy day."

"Amen," Mr. Clarkson said.

"The purser has also been turned over to the Italians, to rest uncomfortably in the jail of the city of Columbus. However, I doubt that he will stay there long. He is wanted, and very widely."

"For murder?" Mr. Clarkson asked.

"Yes, and smuggling opium."

"Which," Owings said, "is the greater crime."

"Ah?" Medford seemed to give the comparison thought. "Yes, I expect you are right. Murder can be committed on impulse; drugs . . ." He shook his head. "Very cold-blooded. Well, Gonzales and Miss Smith return to England with me in"—he consulted his watch—"two hours' time."

"But—opium? The purser?" Mr. Clarkson looked like a small boy pleading for a bedtime tale.

Medford examined the eager face and smiled. He said, "Purser Ernst Herbst and the deceased Dr. Otto Ulmann were two minor cogs in a smuggling ring. The secretary

186

of this line was a slightly bigger cog. How far the chain goes and to whom it stretches will probably be no clearer at the end of this affair than it ever is. Someplace, living in total respectability, donating to charity, bringing his daughters into society, perhaps titled, certainly looked up to, is a gentleman who heads a vast syndicate of drug smuggling. We never catch, never get near him—and the one or two others like him. But we do our best, with the valuable aid of Interpol. Dr. Ulmann, Herr Herbst, and Von Winckel, secretary of this line, were part of the chain. There was a steward at one time, name of Willy Schoeck, who was also a part of that chain. He tried to resign, but one doesn't resign from such a business. He was killed. Then when Dr. Ulmann tried to blackmail for more money, it was decided—by Von Winckel and his superiors —that he too was to be disposed of. The purser was chosen to do the job of work. He was a bad choice, but the only one available. So although he finally bowed to the voice of authority, he waited a hell of a time. Von Winckel had to act before the crime had taken place."

He paused and thought of his morning interviews.

After Medford had visited with Beth Smith, who looked pale but composed, he sought out Frau Schmidt and put a single question to her. Then he went to the purser's cabin door and waited while an Italian policeman unlocked it for him.

The purser, although indisputably green, had recovered enough to take the offensive. "What is that man doing in front of my door?" he demanded as Medford entered.

"The Italian authorities have taken over the ship. That particular one is guarding you."

"Why me?"

"Have you forgotten that you confessed to the attempted murder of the man known as Swendstrom?"

"I did nothing of the sort!"

That was uncomfortably near the truth. Medford said, "But you did kill Dr. Ulmann."

"I?" Fear was so much a normal part of the purser that he didn't seem any more noticeably guilty than usual.

"And," Medford said doggedly, "what about the opium?"

"What opium?"

Medford turned to the Italian policeman and said, more or less in Italian, "What does one do about a search warrant? How do we look for something?"

"Hidden? Here?"

"Most likely."

"Well, we look," said the policeman, seizing the edge of the mattress.

It hadn't taken three minutes, since the box of opium—a large box—was merely locked into a small case that lay under the bed.

The purser folded instantly.

"Why didn't you try to hide it?" Medford asked curiously, looking down on the crumpled purser, who was simply a mass of bones folded awkwardly beneath a woeful face.

"What for? It wasn't mine! I didn't want it! I just wanted to give it to that—that doctor. And then I realized he was a—a fake, so I had no choice but to put the stuff in his liquor, did I?"

"How about throwing it overboard?"

The purser looked shocked. "I had been instructed!" he explained hotly. "I had to follow instructions!"

"Quite. But the man called Swendstrom wasn't so easy to get drunk, eh?"

"It was terrible, just terrible!" the purser said earnestly. "Not at all like Ulmann. Ulmann drank fast, much faster than me."

"Sad," Medford commented. The confession lingered in the air, and Medford's next words had the air of sympathy, of acceptance: "The so-called Swendstrom drove you crazy by not recognizing your signals, by not accepting the drugs, by not understanding?"

"It was terrible!" The purser reached toward the air of sympathy.

"And so you were understandably angry with him." Medford's sympathy was not entirely false. The purser's standards were different than his, different than any Englishman's, different than most people's. By his standards it had undoubtedly been "terrible." Medford said, "And because you were angry, you accused him of pushing his— Miss Smith?"

Herr Herbst set his teeth and looked like an undernourished rat, an undernourished stubborn rat.

Medford said quietly, "You're going to have a lot of trouble on your hands. If the young man pushed Miss Smith, it will have no effect on your troubles one way or the other, and it is best to tell the truth. But if he did not push her—then you will be adding one more complication by adding one more lie."

What penetrated first was the purser's recognition of the fact that he was in trouble. Probably, Medford thought, Herr Herbst, dedicated to the principle of obedience, respectful of Authority to the point of deifying it—probably he had not actually realized until that minute that Authority, even though he considered it entirely to blame and himself entirely guiltless, might not shoulder the punishment. Once, at the collapse of a war, Sergeant Herbst had had a bad time, even though he had been a good and obedient sergeant. The lesson in unfair denouement was about to be repeated. The recognition grew in his eyes, and he abandoned stubbornness for fear.

"The so-called doctor—?" Medford urged gently.

Herbst was a vindictive man, but the possibility that Medford had etched was irresistibly true: an unnecessary lie could only complicate the problems he had just come to recognize as existing. He said, almost absent-mindedly, "She slipped. There was almost no one left in the lounge. She had been looking—peculiar—as if her mind were far away—during the time I examined her passport, and then when she started down the stairs she slipped. A very bad fall."

"Ah."

Medford said to Mr. Clarkson, "This mess is the result of a series of interlocking crises. Von Winckel had a crisis: get rid of Ulmann and replace him. He called on the purser to do the job, and thereby created a crisis for Herbst. Meanwhile Von Winckel chose a replacement who had done smuggling jobs before and could be 'trusted.' A man named Swendstrom. But Swendstrom faced a crisis, too."

Medford paused and looked at Clarkson, then at Owings. He said, "By way of interruption—my confreres in the Yard are very capable chaps. This morning early they had me on the phone, and they also sent much material by mail." He reached in his pocket and brought out a thick sheaf of folded papers. He laid them in front of him on the bar, and said, "Crises. One after another. The Yard explained this morning that in the briefcase that was among the luggage Swendstrom, the real Swendstrom, had packed for the trip on the *Tilburg* was a list of debts. His house was about to be attached, and he could not leave England without giving his wife a sizable amount of money to take care of matters with. So he went to a Dr. Barkland, whom he knew, and who seems to have bowed to a certain amount of blackmail by Swendstrom. Also, and this will interest you, Dr. Owings, it begins to seem likely that Barkland was one of those saints one meets occasionally in your profession. It is very possible that he helped Swendstrom out of kindness rather than out of fear. But when Swendstrom entered Dr. Barkland's office he created, simply by his presence, a triple crisis—for himself, for the doctor, and for the third man who was sitting there. I got some of the story from Gonzales this morning."

"Gonzales?" Mr. Clarkson said.

"Our ship's 'doctor.' He is a stupid man. Constantly does foolish, unthinking things. Once, when he was hiding from

Detroit police, he became a movie actor. How to advertise your whereabouts in one easy lesson."

Owings had been looking down into his glass, but now he looked up and said, as if an enormous problem had been solved, "Ah, the beautiful teeth!"

Medford nodded. "I suppose they were perfected in Hollywood. Quite."

"And," Mr. Clarkson said, "that's why Miss Elkin knew him?"

"Yes, as Robert Ramon, movie actor."

"A movie actor. What do you know?" Owings seemed fascinated by the thought.

"So," Mr. Clarkson said severely, "when he realized Miss Elkin had recognized him, he conked her."

Medford nodded. "Stinking identifiably of a floral cologne. As I said, he is not intelligent, and if nothing else proved it, the bang he gave Miss Elkin would. He doesn't seem really to have wanted to kill her—if so, why not use one of the surgical knives the doctor's office abounds in? But what good would it do to give her a bad headache? A foolish man who acts on impulse is a man doubly silly."

"But," Owings said, "seeing it from Miss Elkin's point of view—she is too kind and too careful to cast accusations about until she is sure."

"Quite." Medford smiled. "Yes, Doctor. Your point about Miss Elkin's honesty was always well taken."

"And Miss Smith is his wife?" Clarkson asked. "During that scene last night—"

"*Was* his wife. She divorced him."

"Just never occurred to me," Max said. "During all the time I spent with her—just never occurred to me. . . . But he attacked her? Pushed her down the stairs?"

"No. She fell. Unaided. He did make those scratches all over her, however. It seems incredible to me, but he apparently didn't realize that the captain would insist that you should examine her. As with Miss Elkin, he didn't really want to hurt her—in point of fact, I suspect he loves her."

"If such a man can love."

"Well," Medford said, "I am not a psychoanalyst."

"Neither—" Max stopped.

"I know. Neither are you. But I suppose, looked at from the human point, your objection has merit."

"Um." Max looked thoughtful. "And scratching her up was his way of keeping her out of sight? Out of circulation?"

"Not exactly. He hoped, Doctor, to keep her out of *your* sight."

Max stared at him.

"Yes. But as is usual with that chap, he got precisely the opposite result."

"But *why?*" Mr. Clarkson asked. "My goodness! What does he say himself, this Gonzales? You've talked to him?"

"Yes," Max said, "this man you call stupid, is he to be trusted? What *does* he say?"

Medford looked at him thoughtfully. "He starts quite a way back. With the murder of Dr. Barkland, and before."

Gonzales—propped up in bed, still in his gaily striped pajamas—was weak, sardonic, apparently unafraid. He behaved, in one way, like the purser and like a great percentage of the criminals who had passed through Medford's hands: Gonzales felt that most of his actions had been quite unavoidable, and that any sensible person would understand how he had been forced to take the actions he took.

Also like the purser, he started off on the offensive. "Come to arrest me for pushing Beth down the stairs?" His expression was derisive.

"Herbst has admitted you didn't. Which doesn't change the fact that you attacked her afterward. Probably with a delicately wielded razor blade?"

"Not true," Gonzales said promptly.

"No? Frau Schmidt is a woman of probity. Spotless record. Not quite like yours, you see. And she says it was your voice on the phone, the call that took her away from Miss Smith's side."

"Reputation or no reputation, her word is unsupported by—"

"In English."

Gonzales looked up at him, apparently thinking as quickly as possible, but that wasn't fast enough and he got angry before he got things sorted. "How did I know the captain was going to insist on having Owings called in? What could I do?" He spread his hands.

"Simple," Medford commented. "Cut her up."

"Very clever remark. But if that Owings hadn't been called in I'd have got away with it, wouldn't I?"

"There's something I don't understand, Gonzales. Explain to me, will you? Were you trying to keep Elizabeth Smith out of the sight of the ship, or out of the sight of Dr. Owings? If it was the latter, you did a remarkable job in reverse—but why? Why didn't you want Owings in contact with her?"

Gonzales looked at him cagily, looked away, and muttered, "Well, if it hadn't been for Owings, I might have got away with it."

Medford thought of the real Swendstrom, of the stethoscope, the fingerprint, of the unceasing work of the laboratory, of the mass of paper that had been sent him that morning—representing hours and hours of man labor—of the Yard's doctors, of Trehane, of himself. He said, "Got away with it? With what? Which offense? Anyway, I doubt that you could have got away with anything, if for no other reason than that there were just too many doctors around."

"What? No, just Owings."

"There was also Dr. Ulmann."

"I had absolutely no connection with that guy."

Medford thought of the superintendent and his stubborn certainty that there was a connection. He had been right in a way, but Medford had been right too, in that the links were not forged but merely contiguous. He said, "Well, you had the unfortunate connection of Ulmann's having been a guinea pig for you. The purser had great success in getting the poison into him, so he tried it out on you."

"*That* character," Gonzales said scornfully. "Couldn't hold his liquor at all. I don't like the stuff but it was easy enough to drink him under the table."

"But with a different potion. And the whole point is that you drank too *slowly*. Oh, well— Look, Gonzales, I say you scratched up your ex-wife. You've just about admitted it. But, you know, I would hardly need that charge."

"No? What the hell else can you charge me with?"

"My goodness," Medford said mildly, "are you serious? Forgetting all current events, how about the Detroit police?"

"I doubt that that little contretemps constitutes an extradictable offense."

"That's an astonishingly fancy sentence. Only one thing wrong with it—your doubt is pure nonsense. Anyway it is likely that English justice will prefer to deal with you itself —charges abound. Upward from attacking Miss Elkin through the murder of Dr. Clarence Barkland and Dr. Nils Swendstrom."

Gonzales stared at him. He said evenly, "You're crazy." Then he cocked one of his handsome eyebrows, and looked wise. "I am an Englishman, you know. My father was naturalized and I was born in Ipswich—"

"Quite. Although I'll never know what you did with your accent. But Ipswich makes it easy; English justice will therefore have first dibs."

Gonzales ignored him. "—and so I understand English law.—You charging me?"

"Not quite yet."

"Because if you are, you are behaving most unethically. No warning, for instance."

Medford stared at him, and then, to his own surprise, he laughed, an entirely natural laugh that sprang from pure amusement. He suddenly understood how this handsome man, with his almost engagingly childish mind, could enthrall and hold a woman like Beth Smith. During his long talk with Miss Smith that morning, Medford had found her down-to-earth and intelligent. Only on the subject of her ex-husband had she been incomprehensible. He began to see why. "As usual," he said, "you've got it backwards. I am permitted to question you *before* I charge you, but not *afterwards*." The reply underlined his growing understanding of Beth Smith's reaction: One was inclined to treat Gonzales almost seriously, with the solemnity one often offered to a five-year-old.

"Well, I didn't kill Barkland or Swendstrom. Nor anyone else. Ever."

"No? But you masqueraded as Swendstrom before it was known that he was dead." Through Medford's mind passed a rapid vivid picture of that stethoscope, so inexplicably tucked into Nils Swendstrom's overcoat pocket. It was a signature, that stethoscope, the signature of a man who would hide from the police by becoming a movie actor. He said, "And you disposed of his body. Tell me, Gonzales, why did you bother to tear out all the labels and then put the clothes back on him? Why bother with clothes at all?"

Gonzales looked up at him with undisguised scorn. "Tch," he said. "I don't know who did it, but if it were I, I shouldn't have wanted to carry a nude body through the streets of London on a Saturday morning."

"Oh. Quite. Sorry. Ashamed of myself." Medford smiled at him.

Gonzales eyed him cagily—a five-year-old sizing up the situation. He said tentatively, "It's all very complicated . . ."

"Uncomplicate it. Start at the beginning."

"Um. That's Barkland. Or Beth."

"Or the Terrence Clinic business?"

"But you must know all about that. That was a kind of a beginning, of course, but all this—all this is really the fault of Beth. She was so stubborn, and so nervous. And all. And Barkland was a good guy, you know. And a good doctor. But then he began to try to prove to her that all she had to do was sort of get over me and she'd be all right." The memory of outrage was reflected on his face. He shook his head. "Can't understand it. He'd always been a good guy. So anyway I forbid her to go see him any more. But when I went round to her flat that Saturday morning she wasn't home, and I knew right away where she was. I went straight to Barkland's, but she had already been and gone. And Barkland was dead. And so was old Swendstrom, whom I hadn't seen since the courtroom, ten years before. And . . ."

"He walked in," Medford explained, "and found mayhem. The murderer was sitting there, more or less surrounded by dead bodies, in a daze, and quite unprepared to do anything whatever about it. He didn't even try to add Gonzales to his harvest of the dead, although he couldn't have succeeded: Barkland's little gun was empty, and Gonzales had thirty-one years to the murderer's forty-one. Anyway, Gonzales, an always willing and immensely haphazard improvisor, took over instantly. He would help, he announced, and the dazed murderer let himself be taken in hand.

"Swendstrom had several motives for this seeming philanthropy. The first of his motives was a strong one. If those two bodies were found there, together, the Terrence Clinic affair would undoubtedly be resurrected, and he was one of that group. And, another tie, his ex-wife had been a patient of Barkland's. Even if he weren't accused of the murders (and he might well have been; he came on the scene seconds after the murders and so could hardly have provided an alibi) he would be sought, and might be found. And, forgetting murder, there were warrants out for his arrest—at least one, in the United States, and I should think a few others under other names. That was his negative, self-protecting motive, and an unusually sensible one. The others were fey, products of his usually silly reasoning: This man was a murderer and could become monetarily helpful. Gonzales himself could get out of London. He could take a nice trip to faraway romantic lands, all expenses paid. He could play doctor, a role he had always fancied himself in, and had even tried to prepare legitimately for before he closed the door forever by becoming a procurer for a group of abortionists.

"So Gonzales took over, and immediately doublecrossed his barely conscious partner. He never mentioned his ex-wife, but removed her file and a number of others while explaining that this would give the police a wrong directional twist. He was merely 'helping.' He then 'helped' by putting Swendstrom's body in his car and dumping it in the Thames—leaving a stethoscope in a pocket. Then—doublecrossing again—he purchased a ticket for Beth Smith. Again his motives were ambivalent—partly he wanted her out of town when the murder was discovered. She was very fond of Dr. Barkland. On the other hand, he didn't want to lose her.—But he didn't mention any of this to the murderer. And the murderer doesn't seem to have asked any questions—an intelligent man, he was in almost total shock, already harvesting the payment that comes to a person who, in a moment of fury, commits murder. So he made only one stipulation—perhaps because he knew a little of the foolishness of Gonzales: 'Get rid of the body, if you want; substitute yourself; take the files; do anything you please, but don't you dare skulk around me in the future.' Probably he had a vivid picture of what the child-brained Gonzales would be like as an accessory after murder. Gonzales quoted him: 'One word from you to me on this whole subject and I will give myself—and you—up to the police.' Gonzales had the sense to believe him, but he didn't have the brains to realize that the murderer just didn't want to talk, to think, to remember. Gonzales thought he was afraid of blackmail, and Gonzales was holding his thunder."

"But," Mr. Clarkson asked, "who was this man?"

"His name is James Bently Fuller."

"What good is Gonzales as a witness?" Max asked. "Will his word stand up in a court?"

"Makes no difference. Once the checking starts and the tracks are uncovered . . ." Medford shook his head. He picked up the sheaf of papers that lay before him, unfolded them and shuffled through. He said, "These are the brought-up-to-date-wherever-possible dossiers on the eleven men who were variously involved in the Terrence Clinic abortion ring. Four are dead—two of natural causes, and Barkland and Swendstrom. And we know all about Gonzales. So that leaves six others. Ah, here it is." He extracted one of the sheets. "This is the story of James Bently Fuller. He was young at the time of the trial, only a little over thirty. He was an American, a New Yorker, a man with, the court was given to understand, a brilliant future. He was in England to study under a famous surgeon, an opportunity given only to the most promising. And yet he got involved in this sordid affair. The judge made quite a speech about Fuller, about his ex-future, its destruction. He sentenced him only to eighteen months—a very moderate punishment. But the big punishment, of course, was the loss of permission to practice. He was struck off in England, and the United States' medical associations followed suit.

"Fuller got the usual time off for good behavior, and so he served only twelve months. But that didn't matter; what mattered was that he—a dedicated surgeon—a doctor—a healer—could no longer do the only thing that mattered to him on this earth: practice his profession.

"He went to the United States."

Medford paused. He put the paper back on the stack.

Owings looked somberly into his almost untouched drink.

Mr. Clarkson looked from one to the other, his childlike blue eyes held wide. He said, "I know good men when I meet them. You are both good men. But, treating a fairytale seriously, as one treats a fairytale, I'll ask one question. The American Government is exclusive about whom it admits. How would he get in?"

"James Bently Fuller was an American citizen, Mr. Clarkson. Born there. The question didn't arise."

"Was? Was?" Clarkson looked relieved. "Then Dr. Fuller is dead?"

"In a manner of speaking. Dr. Fuller entered the Port of New York and disappeared. That is the end of his dossier."

"I don't understand," Mr. Clarkson said forlornly.

"Well, here is another report, on another doctor, on Dr. Maxwell Owings. Dr. Owings was a psychoanalyst, practicing in Wisconsin, a suburb of the largest city of that state, Milwaukee. This report from Wisconsin says that he was a divorcé, a dour man, almost a recluse. He was neglecting, almost ignoring his practice, and no one was very surprised when, about eight years ago, he disappeared, practically overnight. He didn't cut his ties completely; he let it be known that he had gone to New York.

"Then, in New York, Dr. Owings set about respecializing. He was a little old for that—although extremely young-looking, his papers, university degree, medical license, and so forth, showed that he was over forty-two—but he made an astonishingly effective student. Which is not surprising, since he was already a neurosurgeon. He also amused his confreres by having his acquiline nose straightened. He said it was because of a deviated septum, but they were doctors, and they didn't believe him. One young man was so ill advised as to make the joke to Dr. Owings himself. It was an ill-advised joke; Dr. Owings displayed a murderous temper and the young interne was briefly hospitalized as a result. Actually, the young interne was quite wrong: the doctor was not motivated by vanity, not a bit of it. . . . Did you kill Maxwell Owings, Doctor?"

Max looked at him.

"This fairy tale is very long," Mr. Clarkson said. "Too long for a fairy tale. Why would he kill this Dr. Barkland?"

"He explained that to Gonzales. In his first state of shock, in a mood usual at such a time, he wished to defend himself. Gonzales was hardly worthy but the doctor insisted upon pleading his case. He probably believed every word was true—until a few minutes ago."

"He told me," Gonzales said. "He told me why. I didn't ask him. I didn't think that was any place to sit around gabbing, but he insisted on telling me about it. Barkland called Fuller at his hotel the night before, suggested Fuller come round and see him, Barkland, in the morning. Fuller wasn't afraid or disturbed. Doesn't seem to have had the sense to see that it was going to be blackmail. Said Barkland was a nice guy, always had been. And when Fuller got there that morning, Barkland played exactly like that— the nice guy. Said that despite a changed nose and ten years' time he had recognized the picture—a picture that had appeared in a newspaper—and that Fuller had better get out fast, because others might recognize it too. And he mentioned Swendstrom. Fuller said he could barely remember Swendstrom, but while he was trying Swendstrom walked in, and then Fuller had no trouble remembering him. None at all. And it was all very clear. They were going to blackmail him, or expose him. It was like the old shill game—'Wouldn't it be dreadful if my husband walked in?' and then, right on cue, in walks the 'husband.'

"He shot Swendstrom with the little gun in the open drawer right there at his hand. And when Barkland made a move he turned the gun on him. But the gun ran out of bullets. Barkland was dead, and he strangled Swendstrom. He said he didn't know he strangled Swendstrom but a couple of minutes later he saw him lying there and he examined him and he had been strangled. Fuller said"— Gonzales paused and then quoted—"'I suppose I killed them. No—I know I killed them. Didn't I? But I have struggled all my life just to do the work I was born to do, and they were threatening that work. Again, and again.'"

Gonzales thought for a minute, frowning, and then he said, "You know, Barkland *was* a nice guy. If he had called *me* up in such a situation, I would have caught on to blackmail right away, but I'd have been kind of surprised. He was a nice guy."

Medford said, "And there was Gonzales again, as backwards as ever. He seems to get his fingertips on the edge of truth, and then he turns it around. Barkland *didn't* have a thought in his mind except for Owings' welfare. He *was* trying to help him. But Swendstrom, caught in his own predicament, arrived without an appointment, without being expected."

Owings looked almost the age his passport gave him. "I don't believe any of that. And I don't believe that Gonzales' testimony would stand."

"Oddly enough, Doctor, Gonzales hasn't named you, hasn't identified Fuller as being the Dr. Owings on board the *Tilburg*. I have no idea, in view of his foggy manner of thinking, what's behind the omission. Perhaps he's afraid it will make matters worse for him. Perhaps, in his oddly ambivalent way, he is being moved by some instinct of mercy. He will break down eventually, of course."

"But how could he not name him?" Clarkson said in a rising voice. "How could he tell that story and not explain?"

"Very simple. It was 'Dr. Fuller' whom he found in Dr. Barkland's office. 'Dr Fuller' made the confession. 'Dr. Fuller' then walked out into the street and disappeared."

"Well, then?" Mr. Clarkson said. His blue eyes seemed to spark with anger. "Well, then?" he demanded.

"But the man he called 'Dr. Fuller' had appeared in a newspaper picture, and had been recognized by Dr. Barkland as being someone else. So Dr. Fuller had another name. And Gonzales, as muddy a thinker as ever, forgot to omit the details about the nose operation. Dr. Maxwell Owings, over seven years ago in a New York hospital, had a nose operation. And Dr. Owings had his picture displayed in a London newspaper, because of the Lloyd child. There are dozens of such pieces of confirmation. For instance, Dr. Owings once told me, deprecatingly, that he was considered a bright student and always got good grades just because of a knack, a facility for parrotting lectures back on to paper. Well, I didn't believe that—I thought and think it was modesty—but it's interesting to note that the real Dr. Owings got quite *bad* grades, was an unpromising student who always managed barely to scrape through. Only after 'he' showed up in New York, specialized in the field that

Dr. Fuller was already proficient in but had no right, under the name of Fuller, to practice any longer—only then was 'Owings' considered a brilliant student. Now, Dr. *Fuller*, on the other hand, during his undergraduate days, and during medical training"—Medford riffled through the papers that lay before him on the bar—"Dr. *Fuller*—"

"Never mind it," Max said. "Never mind."

Medford dropped the papers. He said quietly, "Most of all, it's the future checking that will supply confirmation. One instance—what is the ex-Mrs. Maxwell Owings going to say when she sees a photograph of the man who so kindly continued her alimony payments? Kindly—or prudently. Would a picture of the current Dr. Owings be identifiable by his university classmates? And—even more damning—would it not be likely that, nose or no nose, a picture would indeed be identified by the people who live in that suburb of Milwaukee? Not as Dr. Owings but as Mr. Fuller—or some other name—who lived among them briefly?"

Max stood up. He said, "Owings killed himself. I found him. I buried him. Nobody missed him. He wasn't a man to be missed. I didn't plan any of it; I am not the kind of man who plans such things. I thought, if I thought at all, that it might have been God's way to give a good doctor a chance to practice by replacing a bad doctor who wasn't practicing. If that's sacrilegious, Mr. Clarkson, for your sake I'm sorry. But *I* believe it—almost."

He paused, swallowed. Then he said, "I'm sorry about Barkland. If all this is true . . ." He swallowed again. "One thing—I wasn't guilty in the Terrence Clinic trial. I wasn't guilty. I was totally guiltless." He walked toward the door, stopped, turned toward Medford and then switched his glance to Clarkson. He said, "Pay for the drinks, will you, Mr. Clarkson?" And he left the bar.

Clarkson looked at Medford with open antagonism. "Can you let him go like that?" he demanded.

"Oh, yes."

"But—he might . . . he might—"

"He can't do either of the things, Mr. Clarkson. The Italian policeman outside understands very thoroughly. He will go to London with me in an hour's time. Before then he will be permitted neither to harm himself nor to escape. Doubt that he'd try to escape, really."

Mr. Clarkson took a deep breath. "Swendstrom. I mean, Gonzales. Gonzales was his patient, at his mercy. He could have . . . couldn't he?"

"No. The practical answer is that the stewardess was in constant attendance. The truer answer is that the doctor cannot give less to a patient than his very best, and anyway I doubt that he would harm anyone unless he was in the grip of his fast and frightening temper."

"Well, I *must* say I am surprised by your acceptance of coincidence. I thought coincidence was suspicious in cases like this?"

"Cases like this are usually rank with suspicious coincidence. This affair is practically unique in not having any that I am aware of. What coincidence do you see?"

"The original Dr. Swendstrom was being rushed onto this ship, this trip, the same ship Dr.—Owings—had a ticket for."

"Ah." Medford fished among his papers. "But Dr. Owings didn't have a ticket for either this ship, or this sailing. Here are facsimiles, sent me this morning, of the tickets of all the passengers who boarded at Southampton. Dr. Owings was booked on this line—after all, it is the best and one of the very few that make the run—but he was scheduled to take the *Hamburg*, which departs Southampton ten days from now. This ship is half-empty, and so when Dr. Owings telephoned the Bond Street office the Saturday before sailing, he was told he could be easily accommodated, switched to the *Tilburg*. He sent his ticket over by messenger and it was revised and returned the same day."

"But he went on trying to cure Miss Smith, and succeeding, although it meant the uncovering of Gonzales, and probably himself?"

"Come, come, Mr. Clarkson." Medford smiled gently at him. "He never guessed for a minute that she had anything to do with Gonzales. He didn't know Gonzales had ever had a wife, he didn't know Gonzales had ever been a movie actor. He didn't know anything at all about Gonzales, except that he had been involved in the Terrence Clinic business, and he knew absolutely nothing about Elizabeth Smith. He kept reporting small facts about Miss Smith to me. To me they were clues, because I knew something of the background; to him they had no personal interest or connection."

Clarkson sighed, and gave in. He said, "I remember now . . ." His voice trailed off.

"What, Mr. Clarkson?"

"Little things. He was reluctant to discuss Milwaukee once, even to name it. He didn't want Miss Elkin to take his picture—"

"Pictures are gone, by the way."

"Gone?"

"Miss Elkin reported the theft of her camera to me this morning. Complete with her roll of film."

"And the doctor took it?"

"I have no idea, Mr. Clarkson. The doctor, the purser, Gonzales. I am not inclined to bother deciding which. Camera is undoubtedly overboard."

"I suppose so. Poor old dear!"

There was a pause. Then Mr. Clarkson said, "I liked him."

Medford noted the past tense and thought it terribly appropriate. He said, "I did too."

"I suppose the moral is that a man must govern his temper."

"That's a bit mild, Mr. Clarkson. But I can give you an even milder one: Too many doctors can poison the soup."

www.ingramcontent.com/pod-product-compliance
Lightning Source LLC
Chambersburg PA
CBHW031419250626
47155CB00004B/1556